Darcy's Yuletide Wedding

By Zoe Burton

Darcy's Yuletide Wedding

Zoe Burton

Published by Zoe Burton/Sweet Escapes Press

Early drafts of this story were written and posted on fan fiction forums in December 2020.

ISBN-13: 978-1-953138-06-4

Acknowledgements

First, I thank Jesus Christ for being my Savior and for giving me the skills to write this story and the words to fill it with. I love you!

Additional thanks go to my dear friends and sisters-at-heart, Rose and Leenie. I'd be lost without you.

To my Patreon Patrons: Thank you for your continued support. There are too many of you now to easily list, but you know who you are. Let me say again that you are The Best Patrons in the entire world!

Table of Contents

Chapter 1

Elizabeth Bennet peered out the carriage window as it slowed to pull into the inn. She could see, amongst the crowd waiting for the conveyance to stop, her four sisters. She smiled and lifted her hand when the youngest, Lydia, noticed her watching and waved, bouncing on her toes and nudging another sister, Kitty. Elizabeth had spent nearly three months in London, assisting her aunt; it seemed her sisters had missed her presence at home.

Within a few minutes, Elizabeth was being handed down from the equipage. She laughed when all four siblings converged on her, all speaking at once in a cacophony of sound.

"Welcome back, Lizzy!"

"We rented a private sitting room and bought you lunch!"

"Welcome home, Dearest. How was your trip?"

"Is our aunt well? Were you able to go to church while you were in town?"

"Thank you, it is good to be back. The trip was not overly taxing – the fine weather we have had played a part in that, I am sure; our aunt is well, and I did get to church, but only once each fortnight; and thank you for the meal." Elizabeth hugged each sister in turn, then suggested they retire to the room the other girls had rented.

Lydia and Kitty led the way up the stairs and into the building, then down the hall to a smallish room at the back of the inn. They were soon followed by a maid, who curtseyed when Lydia informed her of their readiness to eat. The servant curtseyed again and exited, pulling the door shut behind her.

As they waited for the tea service and cold meats and cheeses to be delivered, the girls chatted, sometimes talking over themselves. In due time, the maid and her helper brought the food and beverages. The room became quiet for a short while, as the five satisfied their hunger.

Elizabeth, starting to feel full and full of questions, leaned toward her eldest sister, Jane, who sat at her left side. "Tell me of Mr. Bingley."

Before Jane could reply, Lydia jumped into the conversation. "He has planned a ball for Tuesday next and has invited all of us, you included, Lizzy."

"It is in Jane's honor." Kitty could not allow Lydia to be the bearer of all the good news, it seemed.

Elizabeth's eyebrows rose as she turned her head from her youngest two sisters to look at Jane. "Indeed?"

Her face reddening, Jane took a sip of tea, her eyes averted. "No, I am certain that is not his purpose. He is merely attempting to be a good neighbor, and to keep the promise he made after the assembly last month."

Elizabeth was silent for a moment as she examined what she could see of Jane's features as she sat there looking at her plate. In the end, "Hmm," was all she could manage to say. She looked at the younger girls again. "What other news is there? I understand a militia unit has joined us?"

"Oh, yes. Officers, a whole troop of them!" Lydia's face brightened at the thought.

"Not a whole troop. Some of the soldiers are just that – soldiers – and not officers." Mary sniffed, her nose in the air.

Lydia rolled her eyes. "Well, it surely seemed like it was a whole troop of officers." She grinned again. "They are so handsome in their red coats. Wait until you see them, Lizzy. You will think the same, I am sure."

Mary twisted her lips as though she had something sour in her mouth. "She no doubt will, but at least she will not be forced into company with Lieutenant Wickham."

Kitty gasped. "Oh, yes, Lizzy. You are ever so lucky to have avoided meeting him!" She straightened. "I had no idea a gentleman with such pleasant manners could be so wicked."

Elizabeth leaned forward. "What happened?"

Mary opened her mouth to reply, but Lydia beat her to it. "Mr. Leadbeater caught him cheating at cards and darkened his daylights!"

"Ladies do not speak that way, Lydia!" Mary's shocked reaction resulted in a roll of Lydia's eyes but no apology.

"It is true and you know it." Lydia turned to Elizabeth again. "Lieutenant Denny told me himself. Mr. Wickham was in the habit of gambling with the tradesmen in town. The blacksmith caught him playing with marked cards, and beat him senseless. It was the talk of the town for weeks."

Elizabeth's eyes had gone wide. She looked at Jane, who met her gaze with a solemn expression and a nod. "It is true. It was such a horrible thing. I am certain it was only a misunderstanding, and I am positive Mr. Leadbeater did not intend to harm the lieutenant."

"Oh Jane!" Kitty's loud sigh drew every eye to her. "You always see the best in everyone and never the bad, or the fun!"

"I hardly think one man beating another is fun." Elizabeth patted Jane's hand. "I am certain Jane sees the wrong in it; she knows what is correct and what is not."

Jane's lips lifted in a small smile, though her countenance remained reddened after her sister's thoughtless remarks.

Giving her attention back to the younger girls, Elizabeth inquired further. "What happened then, after the beating?"

"Mr. Wickham was taken back to his quarters, and no one saw him for a few days. Then, we got word that he was dismissed from the militia. Denny said he had been ..." Lydia paused as a look of confusion crossed her face.

Kitty helped her younger sister along. "Court-martialed."

"Yes! Thank you, Kitty!" Lydia turned to Elizabeth again. "Mr. Wickham was court-martialed and drummed out of the militia. No one knows what became of him, though Denny thinks he returned to London."

Elizabeth sat back, her curiosity satisfied. "Well, then. I suppose the county is well rid of him if he was as bad as all that."

"I agree," Jane replied. "He did not set a good example for the boys in the area with that sort of behavior."

"I suppose you are right." Kitty sighed. "But he was ever so handsome, and charming."

Lydia nodded vigorously. "And amiable! Why, I never saw anything but a smile on his face."

"Did anything happen to the blacksmith?" Elizabeth sipped the last of her tea, setting the now-empty cup on the table.

"I do not know, but I do not think so." Mary looked at the other girls, who shook their heads.

"We have not heard of anything. He was in his shop, working at the anvil when we walked past today." Kitty pushed her plate away and stood. "We should probably go home now. Mama will be expecting us."

The sisters agreed as one, and with a flurry of skirts and bonnets and reticules, exited the room and descended the stairs.

"There is Henry, waiting exactly where we told him to." Lydia urged her sisters toward the carriage.

A few minutes later, the Bennet girls were ensconced in the equipage. They laughed and chattered as Henry set the horses in motion. Soon, they pulled into the driveway at Longbourn. They spilled out onto the flagstones, laughing, as their parents came out of the house and down the steps.

"Welcome home, Lizzy!" Thomas Bennet greeted his favorite daughter before her mother could. "I have missed you." He bent to kiss her cheek and to accept a kiss in return.

"Thank you, Papa." Elizabeth glanced up at the house. "It is good to be back."

Bennet's left brow rose. "You did not enjoy your visit with your aunt and uncle?"

"I did." Elizabeth smiled. "The children are lively and entertaining companions, and I was happy to be of service to Aunt and Uncle."

Mr. Bennet tilted his head. "But?" He waited for Elizabeth to form her thoughts and reply. She was the most intelligent of his children, as well as the most discerning.

Elizabeth opened her mouth to speak, closed it again, and then began once more. "The grief that lived in that house was difficult to bear. To lose a child the way they did seemed to devastate them. I had all I could do to keep the young ones from noticing too much."

Bennet sighed and looked down. "This is not the first time it has happened to them. It is terrible when it happens once, but to experience it over and over is excruciatingly painful."

Elizabeth gazed at her father, listening intently. She squeezed his hand. She knew her parents had suffered through several miscarriages after Lydia was born. Before she could say anything, Mrs. Bennet pushed her way between them.

"You have had your opportunity to greet Lizzy; now is mine." The matron rudely elbowed her husband out of the way. She turned to her daughter. "Did you meet any gentlemen in town?"

Elizabeth's jaw dropped for a moment. "Mama, I did not go to town to socialize. I was helping Aunt Gardiner with the children. She suffered a horrible loss."

Mrs. Bennet frowned and looked away briefly, her jaw flexing. She swallowed and then swung her tear-filled gaze back to her daughter. When she spoke again, it was in a softer tone that was tinged with a note of distress. "I know she did, but that does not mean you never ventured from the house."

Elizabeth, seeing that her mother did not wish to speak of Aunt Gardiner's loss, replied as gently as she could. "Actually, it does. We remained at home except for the first day or two after I arrived. Even then, I only walked with the children up and down the street. We saw no gentlemen, at least none who wished to be introduced to us."

The corner of Mrs. Bennet's lips twisted downward. "Hm. Well, there is nothing to be done about it now. Come in and sit down. You can tell us about Madeline while we wait for tea." She waved at her other daughters, indicating they should precede her into the house, then followed them.

Elizabeth and her father stared for a moment, then shook their heads in tandem. He offered his arm and, when she took it, led his second child up the steps and into the house.

The remainder of Elizabeth's day was spent catching up with her family and hearing the neighborhood news.

The following morning, Elizabeth awoke to a pouring rain, which meant she could not partake of her favorite morning activity – walking. She stared out the window and sighed, muttering to herself. "I was looking forward to a nice, long ramble. I have not had one since I went to town." She looked around her room. "I suppose I shall have to see what I can do with my newest ball gown. Perhaps Jane has some ribbons or lace I can add to freshen it." With a longing glance out the window and a hopeful desire for a break in the weather, she got started on her day.

Elizabeth's hope was for naught. The skies poured unceasingly for four days, only stopping just before dawn the day of the ball.

Chapter 2

The Bennet carriage rumbled into the drive at Netherfield. It had no sooner stopped than the door opened on its own and out popped the family patriarch. He stood for a moment, took a deep breath and lifted his eyes to heaven, then brushed at the wrinkles in his suit. He turned back and handed out his chattering wife and each of his daughters, from the eldest to the youngest, in order. That task completed, he offered an arm to Mrs. Bennet and led the family up the stairs.

Elizabeth and Jane linked arms to follow. Mary was alone behind them, and Kitty had paired with Lydia.

Elizabeth could not help teasing her sister when she noticed the usually unflappable Jane twisting and untwisting her pelisse in her free hand. "Are you excited? You will soon be gazing upon the handsome Mr. Bingley, who, if Mama and Lydia are to be believed, planned this ball for you and you alone."

"I confess I am." Jane looked over at Elizabeth for a second before turning her gaze back to the stairs under her feet. "If Mr. Bingley truly did plan this ball for me, he might decide to propose." She paused. "It is a bit too soon for that, I think, but he might ask for a courtship instead."

"Is that why you are nervous?" Elizabeth's brows drew together. "Do you not like him?"

Wide-eyed, Jane snapped her head toward her sister. "Of course I do! Why would you even ask me that?"

Elizabeth pulled back, her brows now rising. "I apologize. Why, then, are you nervous?"

"It is not every day one is proposed to, or even asked to court." Jane looked forward again as they reached the top step. "I do not wish to appear a simpleton, is all. I am afraid of replying ill and making him think I do not care for him." She followed her mother toward the room set aside to hold the ladies' coats and pattens.

A grin lifted the corners of Elizabeth's lips. "Is that all? I am certain you will do very well. I am happy to hear you think so highly of him; I should hate for you to accept a gentleman simply because Mama expects you to."

"I would never do that, and you know it. We have discussed this before." Jane stopped as they arrived at the coat room and turned an earnest eye to her dearest sister. "I care very much for Mr. Bingley. More than any other gentleman I have ever met."

"I am happy to hear it. You deserve the best." Elizabeth's grin softened to a tender smile. On impulse, she hugged Jane before following her into the room.

Several minutes later, after helping Mary repair her hem, the young ladies joined their parents and sisters near the receiving line. With the entire family once again gathered in one place, Mr. Bennet led them to the end of the line, where they chatted with their neighbors while waiting their turn to greet their hosts.

When Jane and Elizabeth finally reached the Bingleys, Elizabeth was elated to see clear admiration in the eyes of her host for her sister. She suppressed a grin as she watched Mr. Bingley as Jane introduced her.

"This is my sister who was in London. Elizabeth, this is Mr. Bingley." Jane gestured toward Lizzy with her hand, but her eyes never left Bingley's.

"I am happy to meet you, Miss Elizabeth." Bingley tore himself away from Jane long enough to make her sister's acquaintance. "I have heard much about you."

"All good, I hope." Elizabeth's eyes twinkled as she teased him.

Bingley laughed. "I heard nothing I can identify as bad, so I guess, yes, it was all good." He jumped and glanced over his shoulder at the thin blonde woman beside him. "Please allow me to introduce you to my sister. She is my hostess while I am here at Netherfield." Turning to the woman, he gestured to Elizabeth. "Caroline, this is Miss Bennet's sister, Miss Elizabeth Bennet. Miss Elizabeth, this is my sister, Miss Bingley."

Caroline looked Elizabeth up and down and with a sneer, returned her guest's curtsey with a shallow one of her own. "Welcome to Netherfield, Miss Elizabeth."

"Thank you. I am pleased to be here." Elizabeth was put instantly on guard when she saw her hostess' smirk. Though Mr. Bingley was an amiable, pleasant fellow, it was clear his sister was the opposite. Still, it was not in Elizabeth's nature to be childish, so she merely smiled at the other woman and went her way.

Elizabeth and Jane began to stroll from the receiving line to the ballroom, admiring every inch of the lavishly decorated home. They wandered at leisure down the long room, pausing now and then to speak to a neighbor or other acquaintance.

It was during one of those long pauses that Elizabeth, having spoken to Mrs. Goulding and Lady Lucas and now waiting for Jane to finish speaking so they could move along, saw a tall, elegant, somber young man enter one of the doorways nearest her position. Her eyes caught the gentleman's and held, and the feelings that arose in her breast were like nothing she had felt before. She could not tear her gaze away. She did not know how long she stood there, looking deep into his eyes, but at some point, he seemed to startle and then, with the slightest lifting of his lips, he bowed to her.

It was that movement that snapped Elizabeth out of her stare. She felt a fiery blush rise from her neck to her hairline, but she smiled back and curtseyed. She held her breath when it looked as though the gentleman might walk in her direction, but instead, he moved off to his left and continued on down the room.

"Lizzy, are you well?"

Jane's voice in her ear brought Elizabeth's head around. "I am." She swallowed and looked toward her feet, brushing her hands down her skirt. "Did you see the gentleman who just entered the ballroom? Do you know who he is?"

"I did not. I am sorry." Jane noticed her sister's focus further down the room and looked that direction to see if she could identify the man. "Which one?"

Elizabeth sighed. "He is gone now."

"Describe him. Perhaps I can ask Mr. Bingley to introduce you."

Elizabeth shook her head. "No. If the gentleman wishes for an introduction, he will get one himself. I will not chase him."

Jane looked skeptical. "If you say so."

"I do." Elizabeth pulled in a deep breath. She opened her mouth to say more, when she was interrupted by her friend, Charlotte Lucas.

"Lizzy, welcome back!" Charlotte approached with her hands out, and when Elizabeth grasped them with her own, Charlotte pulled her close for a peck on the cheek as she squeezed her friend's hands.

A warm smile lifted Elizabeth's lips. "Thank you. It is so good to see you! How have you been?"

"The same as always, I am afraid." Charlotte laughed. "Little new happens around here. Mr. Bingley arrived, of course, but you know who snapped up his attention." She winked at Jane, then laughed when the object of her tease blushed a deep red. "His friend, Mr. Darcy, is not as amiable and has not displayed interest in any of the local ladies, and the officers ended up being either married or wastrels." She shrugged.

"I am sorry. That *is* one of the negative things about living in Meryton; new gentlemen rarely visit." Elizabeth sympathized with her friend's feelings.

Charlotte changed the subject. "I understood your cousin, the heir, was to visit this week?"

Jane spoke up. "He was supposed to, but Papa received a letter the day he should have arrived stating that he had been forced to put off the visit until at least Epiphany. He has been ill, it seems, and unable to travel."

"Well," Elizabeth inserted, "based on the ridiculousness of his letter, I daresay it is no terrible tragedy that his visit has been delayed. I know Mama is relieved, though she was unaware that Mr. Collins was even planning to visit."

Charlotte chuckled. "Did your father wait to tell her until the last minute?"

"He did! He announced at breakfast that the man was due that afternoon, and then at tea time, read us the letter canceling the trip." Elizabeth shook her head and rolled her eyes as she started to laugh.

"I can see Mr. Bennet taking great enjoyment in that."

"He did." Jane giggled. "He sat down while Mama expressed herself and laughed for the longest time."

At that moment, a short, solidly built young man joined the ladies. "What are you girls laughing about?"

"We were talking about Mr. Bennet gaining enjoyment from vexing his wife." Charlotte nudged the newcomer with her elbow. "Are you not going to greet Lizzy, Brother?"

"I am, if you will give me a few moments." The gentleman looked from Charlotte to Elizabeth. He bowed to her. "Welcome back to Meryton, Lizzy. It is good to have you back."

Elizabeth laughed and curtseyed. "Thank you, Stephen. I am happy to have returned."

Stephen smiled but did not reply. Instead, he inclined his head toward his sister. "Mama insisted I dance the first with you. She has convinced Papa to do the same with her." He held his elbow out toward Charlotte as the musicians began to warm up.

"I thought she might." Charlotte shrugged and tucked her hand under Stephen's arm. "I suppose a dance with my brother is better than none at all. Lizzy, Jane, I will catch up with you later. Perhaps we can eat together, if none of us has been asked to dance the supper set."

"Yes, we can." Elizabeth smiled. "Enjoy your dance." She waved her friend and her brother away as Mary stepped beside her.

"Lizzy, has anyone asked you or Jane to dance?"

"No; not yet, anyway. Has anyone asked you?" Elizabeth was distracted by the sight of three gentlemen who seemed to be approaching her and her sisters.

"No." Mary's gaze followed Elizabeth's. "Who are they?"

"I recognize Mr. Alexander Tillet. The gentlemen with him must be his brothers, Mr. Basil Tillet, and Mr. Jerome Tillet. They are cousins to the Gouldings." Elizabeth stopped speaking as the trio of gentlemen stopped in front of her. She joined her sisters in curtseying when the men bowed.

"Good evening, ladies." Alexander Tillet, the eldest of the three, greeted the Bennets. "My brothers and I noticed that you do not appear to have partners for the first set. We should be honored to dance with you." His brothers nodded in agreement with his words.

"If you will have us." Jerome, the youngest of the young men, squeaked the words. He pulled at his cravat and blushed when three female pairs of eyes turned his way.

Elizabeth glanced at Mary, who nodded, and then at Jane. She tilted her head at her elder sister to give her a silent response.

Jane lifted her lips as she replied to Alexander. "We shall be happy to dance with you and your brothers. Thank you for asking."

With a grin, the eldest Tillet brother offered his arm to Jane. As he began to walk her toward the line of dancers, Basil and Jerome followed suit, Basil with Elizabeth and Jerome with Mary.

The set passed quickly. Elizabeth found Basil Tillet to be an interesting, if pompous, fellow who was studying law, had plans to become a judge, and held country solicitors in contempt. By the end of the first dance, Elizabeth had dismissed him entirely as a possible husband. She could not marry a gentleman who looked down on her uncle, especially when that gentleman was, essentially, in the same trade. She remained polite, however. It was not in her nature to be rude, despite the provocation. A few well-placed comments, ones that sailed right over his head, were revenge enough.

When the set ended, the Tillet brothers returned the Bennet sisters to their mother's side. They bowed and moved away to find other partners. Elizabeth turned to Jane and Mary and opened her mouth to ask them their opinions of their partners when Mr. Bingley approached. She smiled in delight, covering with her hand the giggle that arose when Jane instantly became coquettish.

"Oh, Mr. Bingley!" Mrs. Bennet drew her host's attention. "How well you look tonight. The ballroom is decorated to perfection, as well."

"Thank you." Bingley looked around the room. "My sister outdid herself. I will be certain to pass your compliments on to her."

Mrs. Bennet preened, lifting her chin proudly with a smug smile.

Bingley turned to Elizabeth. "There is someone who wishes to meet you, Miss Elizabeth." He stepped back half a pace and gestured to someone standing behind and to the side of him. "May I introduce him?"

"Of course." Elizabeth's countenance displayed her delight. She loved to meet new people.

"Miss Elizabeth Bennet, please meet Mr. Darcy of Pemberley in Derbyshire. Darcy, this is Miss Elizabeth Bennet of Longbourn."

Elizabeth's welcoming smile had frozen on her face as she caught sight of the gentleman, who had earlier caught her attention, bowing to her. Bingley's words seemed to come to her from far away. She curtseyed in automatic response to her new acquaintance's greeting, her eyes flying up to his as she arose.

Her heart pounded as she recognized the interest in his eyes. She could not pull her gaze away from his dark brown orbs. She shivered when his deep voice reached her ears.

"I am pleased to make your acquaintance, Miss Elizabeth. Would you care to dance the next with me?"

Elizabeth stammered as her mind struggled to catch up with her mouth. "I-, I would. Thank you." She was fascinated by the tiny lifting of the corners of his lips and the way it softened the expression on his face. She startled when he held his elbow out to her. "Oh." She swallowed and curved her hand around his forearm. A jolt traveled from her fingers to her heart, and she wondered if he felt it, as well.

Chapter 3

Silently, the pair made their way to the newly-formed line of dancers. Elizabeth was, uncharacteristically, unable to find something to talk about. She had never felt the emotions before that she felt now, in the gentleman's presence, and she was uncertain what to say. Darcy escorted her to the line of ladies and bowed slightly before stepping to the gentlemen's side. She shook herself, closing her eyes and feeling the rise of the courage that always sustained her in uncertain situations.

"Mr. Bingley said you are from Derbyshire?" Elizabeth asked the question once her partner had taken his place and turned to face her.

"I am."

Darcy's low-pitched voice washed over her, making her quiver inside. She tilted her head. "One of my aunts lived in Derbyshire for a few years in her youth. She has nothing but praise for the scenery there."

Darcy lifted one corner of his lips. "It is beautiful country, full of hills and gorges and escarpments."

"According to my uncle, there is also a great deal of very good fishing to be had." Elizabeth's eyes twinkled. "He was an avid fisherman in his youth. He and my aunt visited the Peak District during their wedding trip several years ago. He often tells rather interesting tales about the number and size of the fish he caught that week."

Darcy chuckled. "I can imagine. I have stories of my own, as do many of the men who grew up there."

Elizabeth shook her head, but was unable to say more for the time being, as the dancing had commenced, and her attention was taken by the complicated first steps. Soon, she and Darcy had taken hands and twirled and now promenaded hand in hand down the line. "Do you have any family, Mr. Darcy?"

"I do. I am guardian to my young sister, and I have aunts, uncles, and cousins in London and Derbyshire." Darcy glanced at Elizabeth, his gaze seemingly also riveted to its partner. "I believe Bingley told me you recently returned from London?"

"I did. I was helping my aunt and uncle with their children. My aunt was unwell for a while and the nursery maid was overwhelmed with two rambunctious children under the age of seven." Elizabeth stepped forward as the dance required and took Darcy's hands.

"Your aunt prefers to be directly involved with her children?" Darcy turned his partner in a circle then held her hand as they promenaded again.

"She does. She adores children in general, and is very good with them. She usually takes the older one out of the nursery in the mornings and walks with him or plays games designed to teach him his letters and numbers and things. Then, she takes him back upstairs for a mid-day meal and puts the pair of them down for naps so the maid can take a break." Elizabeth shrugged. "They have considered hiring a second nursery maid, but my aunt gets so much enjoyment out of her involvement that they have not."

"I admire her for her choice. My mother was that way, as well. Too many of my friends and acquaintances have not had that deep connection with their parents that I had and they have suffered for it. It is unpopular in the higher circles of society to be so, to their own detriment." Darcy let go of Elizabeth's hand and they stepped to their respective sides.

"Are you close to your mother?" Elizabeth's gaze locked onto Darcy's once more, and it seemed he was similarly inclined to look at her, for he never looked away.

"I was. Sadly, my mother passed away when I was four and ten."

Elizabeth heard a note of melancholy in Darcy's voice. "I am so sorry. That is a tender age for a boy to lose a parent."

"It was difficult. I miss her still. I see her, though, when I look at my sister, for Georgiana is the picture of our mother." Darcy smiled softly. "She sounds like Mother some-times, too."

"You are close to your sister, then? You said you are her guardian?" Elizabeth found her hand itching to join with Darcy's once again. She held both tightly to her sides as she waited their turn, to keep herself from reaching for him.

"I am. I share the responsibility with one of my cousins. My sister is more than ten years my junior. She is currently staying with my aunt and uncle in London. I hope to bring her to Netherfield for Christmas." Darcy had relaxed as he spoke of his sibling, his countenance reflecting the tender feelings he had for her.

"She must not be very old, then?" Elizabeth continued to draw Darcy out. She was fascinated with this softness he displayed for his family.

"She is fifteen. We took her out of school in the spring." Darcy's countenance suddenly darkened. "We sent her on holiday to Ramsgate, but she is back in town now."

Elizabeth looked down, biting her lip. It was clear that something about his sister's visit to the seaside town had not gone well. Knowing how Lydia, who was also fifteen, could behave, Elizabeth could sympathize with Darcy's feelings. She cast about for a different topic. "Do you enjoy reading?"

After a startled look, Darcy's features relaxed. "I do. The libraries at my estate and my house in town are both extensive." He tilted his head. "Do you?"

Elizabeth grinned for a moment before schooling her features. "I do. My poor father has all he can do to keep me in new reading material. I have read everything in his library, or nearly so."

"What sorts of books do you read?" Darcy reached for Elizabeth's hands again, as their turn had arrived once more.

Elizabeth happily slipped her hands into Darcy's, marveling to herself at how warm and comforting the feel of his palms were. "Oh, anything I can get my hands on, though my preference is for poetry and histories. I also enjoy a good novel now and again, just for variety."

Darcy chuckled. "I appreciate variety, as well, though I rarely read novels. I am obliged to occasionally, when Georgiana requests permission to read one, but I do not make them part of my daily study."

"What about poetry?" Elizabeth looked up at Darcy from the corner of her eye as they circled.

"Poetry is not my favorite thing to read, but I do enjoy Burns and Wordsworth now and then." Darcy smirked. "I much prefer anything Shakespeare to poetry."

"Oh, the Bard!" Elizabeth sighed. "Now there is a gentleman who knew how to write. He is a favorite of mine."

"Do you prefer his histories, his comedies, or his tragedies?" Darcy cocked his head to the side as he watched her, paying no attention at all to where he was walking.

"Oh, his comedies for sure. I dearly love to laugh." Elizabeth spoke over her shoulder as she moved back into position on the ladies' side of the line.

Darcy chuckled again. His gaze moved up and down Elizabeth's form, dark eyes glittering. "I am not surprised. You have been uniformly cheerful this entire dance, and the ribbons on your gown are a lovely, bright color."

Elizabeth blushed, looking down at her white gown and smoothing her hand down the lavender-colored ribbon that trailed from just under her bodice to nearly her knees. "Thank you." She looked back up to find his eyes focused on hers once more. "Purple is my favorite color, and I try to add a shade of it to every gown in some manner." She looked down again. "It is silly, I know, but it pleases me and is not hurtful to others, so I continue."

"I do not think it silly at all. My sister loves pink; she has pink on everything she owns. If she could complete her correspondence on pink paper and write with pink ink, I think her life would be complete." Darcy rolled his eyes, but his smirk demonstrated his amusement.

Elizabeth laughed, lifting her hand over her mouth. "You are undoubtedly correct. I feel the same about purple, though I do not share that information around." She shook her finger at Darcy. "So do not go telling anyone I said it. I will roundly deny it if you do."

It was Darcy's turn to laugh. "I will not." He turned his head toward the orchestra as the first dance ended and the second was called. This dance was a jig, which made conversation more difficult.

When the set was over, Darcy once again offered his arm to Elizabeth. "May I get you a glass of punch? That was a long set of dances; you must be as parched as I am."

"Please do, thank you." Elizabeth held tightly to Darcy's arm as he led her to the table of refreshments. They were soon joined by Bingley and Jane.

"What an invigorating set that was! Do you not agree, Darcy?" Bingley, always cheerful and buoyant, fairly bounced when he spoke.

"I daresay it was. I cannot think when I have enjoyed a set more." Darcy did not look at his friend when he spoke. Instead, his gaze was focused on Elizabeth.

Bingley slapped Darcy on the shoulder. "I am happy to hear it. You should dance more often. Perhaps now you will." With a wink, he pulled Jane away.

Darcy shook his head at his friend's words. He accepted the empty cup Elizabeth handed him and held his arm out to her again. "Shall we find a quiet corner and rest for a few minutes?"

Elizabeth smiled up at her partner. "I would like that." She tucked her hand under his elbow once more, feeling again the tingle shooting straight to her heart. She strolled beside him as he made his way toward the corner of the ballroom.

"There are two empty seats near that door." Darcy leaned his head down to speak. "They are within sight of anyone who wishes to see but are also set apart, which will give us a modicum of privacy. They will be sufficient for our needs, I should imagine."

Elizabeth rose up on tiptoes to look at the chairs Darcy indicated. Putting her heels back on the floor, she nodded. "They will do very well, I think."

With a nod and a quick lifting of the corners of his lips, Darcy began to move toward the empty seats. Soon, he was assisting Elizabeth down into one and pushing the other closer to her.

Elizabeth straightened her skirt as she waited for Darcy to seat himself. Her heart pounded, excitement making her hands sweat inside her gloves. She smiled at him when he spoke.

"Tell me more about your aunt and uncle in London. I understand they live in Cheapside?" Darcy's hand gripped the arm of his chair.

Elizabeth was quick to correct his statement. "They live *near* Cheapside. My uncle designs and manufactures custom firearms. From the top floor of his house, he can see the top of his warehouse."

Darcy's brows drew together. "He is a gunsmith? What was his name, again?"

"His name is Gardiner." Elizabeth tilted her head, watching Darcy's eyes widen and his jaw drop.

"*Edward Gardiner* is your uncle? Miss Bingley did not tell me that. He is very good at what he does."

With a smug smile, Elizabeth agreed. "He is. He is very popular amongst the gentlemen of the *ton*."

"That he is!" Darcy shook his head. "I have heard his employees do all the work, except for the actual designs." He chuckled. "My uncle was quite put out with him. He requested a meeting so he could order a personalized set of dueling pistols, and Gardiner refused to come. He sent his superintendent instead."

Elizabeth laughed. "He has done that to several people, including Prinny. He insists it has made him more popular."

"It may have." Darcy shook his head. "When something is difficult to obtain, a gentleman will go to great lengths to get it. Many have tried and will continue to try to get personal service from your uncle. As long as he continues to produce an excellent product, he will have plenty of business."

Elizabeth's eyes twinkled. "I will be sure to tell him you said that." She laughed when Darcy rolled his eyes. "Turnabout is fair play, you know. Tell me about your uncle, the one with whom your sister is currently residing."

Darcy smiled. "He is an earl. He holds the Matlock seat." He tilted his head, his eyes wandering off into space for a moment. "He is ... forceful, bombastic, and arrogant, but he has a heart of gold. He is my mother's brother and I am told she could be the same in certain circumstances."

"The Earl of Matlock is your uncle?" At Darcy's nod, Elizabeth continued. "He is frequently in the papers. He seems to give many speeches in Parliament."

Darcy chuckled. "He does like to speak, to anyone who will listen. My aunt often must beg him to be silent, to save her tired ears."

Elizabeth's hand lifted to cover her mouth, and her giggle. "My father has been known to do that to my mother now and again."

Darcy's countenance took on an odd expression. "I can well imagine. Your mother is often ..."

"Excessively enthusiastic?" Elizabeth's left brow rose.

"Yes, that is it exactly." Darcy's shoulders slumped for a brief second.

"Mama does not control herself, I know." Elizabeth looked down. She supposed it was best to get this topic out of the way now, rather than later. "It can be embarrassing at times, but she means well."

Darcy said nothing, merely nodding at Elizabeth's words. The couple sat in silence for a moment. Finally, Darcy cleared his throat. "It would be impolite to keep you from dancing with others." He nodded in the direction of a young man who was making his way toward them. "Will you save the supper set for me?"

Elizabeth's eyes widened. Asking a lady to dance two sets was almost making a declaration. However, Elizabeth could not ignore the pull this gentleman had on her. "Yes, I will."

With a quick glance behind her, Darcy swiftly made a second request. "May I call on you tomorrow?"

"Miss Elizabeth." The young man arrived in front of them and bowed. "May I request your hand for this set?"

Elizabeth smiled at the newcomer, then turned to Darcy. "You may." She smiled at him, too, before standing and accepting the arm of the other man. "I look forward to our set, Mr. Darcy." She curtseyed and allowed her new partner to lead her to the dance floor.

Chapter 4

The next day, Elizabeth and her family, like the others in the neighborhood, slept late. They had not arrived home until nearly dawn, so it was noon before anyone in the house stirred.

The day was beautiful, so Elizabeth did what she always preferred to do upon rising. She took a brisk walk along the paths that circled Longbourn. The exercise allowed her to remain in good physical condition – she was rarely ill – and it gave her the peacefulness she needed to organize her thoughts, which were full of Mr. Darcy this morning.

Elizabeth was filled with excitement. She hoped her favorite dance partner from the night before did call on her today. She had vivid memories of the feelings his touch engendered in her, even through the gloves they both wore. *He made my heart sing!* She laughed out loud and turned back toward the manor house, wishing to be ready in case he visited.

When she stepped into the house, Elizabeth could hear her sisters upstairs. She glanced up as she passed the grand staircase on her way to the dining room, but did not see them.

Mary could be heard in the back drawing room, practicing a somber tune on the pianoforte. Elizabeth shook her head at her next youngest sister's choice. It was typical of Mary's taste in music, but was opposite Elizabeth's own.

Jane and Mrs. Bennet were already seated with cups of tea and plates of ham and eggs in front of them when Elizabeth entered the room. She greeted them cheerfully, as she headed to the sideboard to select her favorites from the many choices available. She chose to sit beside Jane and set her plate on the table before sitting down. "How did you sleep?"

Jane paused the motion of her fork. "I slept very well. I have not been so tired in an age." She began eating once more.

"It was a long night, was it not?" Elizabeth grinned as she added a thick layer of cream to a scone. "I have not shared so many dances with gentlemen since I do not know when." She reached for the jar of jam and began slathering some on top of the cream.

"Must you rattle on so?" Mrs. Bennet gripped her head between her hands, her elbows on the table. The housekeeper brought in a steaming mug of coffee, setting it on the table in front of the mistress. Mrs. Bennet snatched up the mug and, holding it in both hands, began to sip.

Elizabeth winced. She decided against asking her mother how she slept, since the lady clearly was unwell. Instead, she silently tucked into her own meal.

Soon, Lydia and Kitty clambered down the stairs and joined the rest of the ladies of the house in breaking their fast. They tumbled into the dining room in their usual fashion, chattering like magpies. At a rebuke from their mother, their loud conversation became whispers. They filled their plates and plopped down into seats at the table.

"La, Lizzy, you were popular last night." Lydia spread butter on her toast. "I do not think you sat out so much as one set. You even danced with Stephen Lucas!"

Elizabeth lifted her shoulders. "I did not sit out. It was an unusual night, to be sure." She smirked. "As for Stephen, I think Charlotte forced him to dance with me, somehow. You know how he hates the activity."

"You danced twice with Mr. Darcy!" Kitty looked up from her eggs and ham. "He never danced with anyone at the assembly who was not of his own party. Is that not right, Lydia?" She jabbed her elbow into her younger sister's side.

"Ow! Stop that!" Lydia rubbed her ribs with one hand as she turned her attention back to Elizabeth. "I almost forgot about Mr. Darcy. You did dance twice with him! Was he a bore?" Lydia ignored her meal and her bruised side to focus her attention on her elder sister. "He has been so cold and arrogant the whole time he has been at Netherfield, but with you he was warm and inviting. What did you do to him?"

Elizabeth swallowed and dabbed at her lips with her napkin. "I did nothing to him. We saw each other while Jane and I were speaking to Lady Lucas and then he asked Mr. Bingley for an introduction. When he requested a dance, I accepted."

"You were sitting over in the corner with him for a while." Lydia teased Elizabeth in a sing-song voice. "What were you doing over there?"

Elizabeth pressed her lips together. "We were talking about our families. His uncle is an earl. The Earl of Matlock." Seeing blank looks in the younger girls' eyes, as well as her mother's, and only mild interest in Jane's, she sighed to herself. "He gives many long speeches in Parliament. Mr. Darcy says he enjoys talking."

"Oh." The confusion in Lydia's eyes, as well as those of the other ladies, cleared. "I noticed you gave him the supper set, too, which means you sat and ate with him. What did you speak about?"

Tartly, Elizabeth responded. "I do not know how you would have seen what I was doing, given you were running around with Lieutenant Denny's sabre."

Lydia had the sense to look embarrassed. "We were not talking about me." She sipped her tea. "I know what the problem is." She set her cup back into its saucer. "You can dish out a tease, Lizzy, but you cannot take one."

Elizabeth inhaled and opened her mouth to reply when Mr. Bennet appeared at the end of the table.

"It is far too early in the day for an argument. We are all undoubtedly fatigued." He looked at his wife at the other end of the table, still nursing her cup of coffee with her eyes closed and her elbows on the table. "Some of us more than others." He looked at his daughters again. "We must, therefore, make allowances with each other."

Elizabeth looked down at her hands, which were clasped together on her lap. "You are correct, Papa." She looked up. "I apologize. To you too, Lyddie. I am sorry."

Lydia sniffed. "I forgive you. And, Papa, I am sorry, as well." She batted her lashes at her father, knowing he would simply roll his eyes and ignore her.

True to form, Bennet shook his head and wandered to the sideboard. Breakfast continued in near silence. After eating, the family separated for a few hours to mostly individual activities. Elizabeth laid down for a nap and dreamt of Mr. Darcy.

As the time for visits approached, the Bennets began to stir again, gathering in the front parlor as a family. Mrs. Bennet, who had also gotten a few more winks, seemed much happier and more amiable.

Elizabeth fidgeted on the sofa beside Jane. So nervous was she that she failed to notice the signs that Jane was hiding something. With a sly smile, the latter finally reached over and laid her hand atop one of Elizabeth's, to prevent the younger girl from continually pressing at the crease in her gown.

"What is the matter, Lizzy? You seem unsettled."

Elizabeth looked at the floor in front of her and puffed out her cheeks. She met Jane's eyes. "I confess I am. Mr. Darcy asked to call on me today." She drew in a deep breath and exhaled. "I so hope he does."

"If he said he would, I am certain he will." Jane patted her sister's hand before drawing her own back to hold the embroidery hoop that had rested in her lap the last few moments. "I am quite positive he will arrive with Mr. Bingley."

Elizabeth's brows shot up. "You are so certain Bingley will come to Longbourn today?"

Her eyes focused now on the needlework in her hands, Jane allowed a mere hint of a smile to lift her lips. "I am." She shot a glance at her sister out the side of her eye but remained silent.

Elizabeth's eyes narrowed as she worked out the meaning of Jane's behavior. Suddenly, they widened. She grasped the other girl's hand, halting her progress mid-stitch. "Jane!" Her voice was a harsh whisper. "Did Mr. Bingley propose to you last night?"

Jane's lips twitched. "He did not." She calmly resumed her activity.

Elizabeth leaned closer. "He requested a courtship?"

Jane looked at her sister again, out the corner of her eye, then winked and looked back at her hoop. She grinned when Elizabeth quietly whooped in her ear.

"Congratulations! I am so happy for you." Elizabeth quickly hugged Jane. She resumed her place before Mrs. Bennet could notice, picking up the book she had dropped on the seat. "He must ask Papa?"

"Yes," Jane murmured. "We wished to savor the news between us before we made any sort of announcement."

"Very wise." Elizabeth opened her book, but stared blankly at the page. "I hope he comes quickly and brings his friend with him."

A quarter hour later, Elizabeth's every wish came true. Mrs. Hill knocked on the drawing room door and, when granted permission to enter, stepped inside to announce Mr. Darcy, the Bingleys, and the Hursts. The Bennet ladies stood and curtseyed while the visitors bowed.

"How good it is to see you!" Mrs. Bennet welcomed the visitors. "Please, do be seated. Lizzy, move over there so Mr. Bingley can sit with Jane."

"Actually, I wish for a moment of time with Mr. Bennet first, if I might." Bingley looked around the room for Longbourn's master as he escorted his sister to a chair.

"He is in his book room." Mrs. Bennet sniffed. "He said something about ledgers but he is probably just reading. I will ring for Mrs. Hill to show you the way."

"Very good, ma'am." Bingley's attention was already caught by Jane. He moved toward her, grasping her hand and bowing over it. "Miss Bennet."

Jane blushed and curtseyed a second time. "Mr. Bingley. It is a fine day today."

Bingley winked. "It is, indeed. Perhaps when I return, we may walk in the garden?"

"I would like that very much." Jane smiled.

"Here is Mrs. Hill." The mistress hurried to her housekeeper. "Mr. Bingley wishes to speak to Mr. Bennet. Please take him there."

Mrs. Hill curtseyed and gestured to Bingley to follow her. Mrs. Bennet immediately turned to Jane.

"Is there something I should know?" A wide smile and large eyes gracing her face, the matron hurried to her eldest daughter.

"No, Mama." Jane's serene smile gave nothing away.

Mrs. Bennet huffed. "Well, I never." She moved to a nearby chair and plopped into it. "What can they be talking about? I thought for sure ..." She became lost in thought as she tried to work out what was going on.

Darcy had, immediately upon being invited to sit, taken up the place next to Elizabeth on the settee to which she had moved to make room for Bingley. Now, he leaned over and spoke in a low tone to his seat-mate. "I believe your mother has completely forgotten my presence." His lips twitched.

"I suspect you are right." Elizabeth's gaze flitted from Darcy to her mother and back. "I apologize for her."

Darcy leaned back. "Think nothing of it. The inducements for accepting her behavior increase by the day."

Elizabeth's lips lifted slightly. "Indeed?" Her heart had yet to cease the pounding that had begun the moment Darcy entered the room. She was eager to touch him, to see if the same sensation zapped her that she had felt last night. To prevent such a forward thing, she kept her fingers clasped tightly around the book she had forgotten to put down.

Darcy noticed the tome. He tilted his head as though to examine the title. "What are you reading?"

Elizabeth looked down. She unclenched her fingers and lifted the book so Darcy could see the front. "*As You Like It.*"

"In the mood for a good laugh?" Darcy's smirk transformed his usually sober countenance.

Elizabeth's heart skipped a beat. *Oh, my,* she thought. She cleared her throat. "Always."

Just then, Bingley returned to the drawing room behind Mr. Bennet. He skirted around his host to take up a place beside Jane as the elder gentleman asked for his wife's attention. Darcy, the Hursts, and the ladies all stood.

"I have news, Mrs. Bennet. Mr. Bingley has asked to court Jane, and I have granted my permission." Bennet bowed to his daughter and her suitor. "Not that it was required, since Jane is of age and had already granted him the honor, but it is in his favor that he held to convention in such a way."

Mrs. Bennet heard nothing beyond the word "court." "I knew it!" Her screech caused everyone in the room to wince, and a few to cover their ears. "Jane, you sneaky child!" She shook her finger at her eldest. "How could you hide such a thing from me?"

Elizabeth watched with a tender expression. She looked up when Darcy's soft, deep voice sounded near her ear.

"You are not surprised by the news?"

"No." Elizabeth shook her head with a smile, looking back at her sister and the rest of her rejoicing family. "Jane told me before you arrived." She chuckled. "I suspect she simply wished to string Mama along for once. Jane has a sly sense of humor." She laughed and turned back to Darcy.

Elizabeth's private conversation with Darcy was interrupted by Caroline Bingley.

"What a waste." Caroline slid her arm into Darcy's as she stepped up beside him. She watched her brother accept the congratulations of the Bennet ladies and curled her lip. Ignoring Elizabeth's presence, she leaned into Darcy's side and turned a coy gaze up at him. "Surely you see the inequity here, Mr. Darcy? Perhaps you can speak to him; convince him of his folly in pursuing a poor country chit."

Elizabeth's mouth fell open for a moment as she listened to Caroline Bingley insult her dearest sister. She stiffened, preparing to demand respect for Jane, if not the entire Bennet family. Before she could open her mouth, a red-faced Darcy spoke.

"Beware of what you say, madam. The sister of the lady in question stands here before you. Surely, even you would not wish to insult the family of the woman who may just be your own sister one day." Darcy pulled his arm away from Caroline's grasping fingers. "It is not up to me to sway Bingley one direction or the other. I can state with certainty that

Miss Bennet is not like the other young women your brother has been enamored of. She is genuine in her affection for him."

Caroline gritted her teeth and leaned forward, still not acknowledging Elizabeth's presence. "She will accept him because her mother expects her to."

Darcy stepped back, stopped only by the edge of the settee behind him. "Untrue. I heard from Miss Bennet herself, when she was unaware I was nearby, that she will not marry simply to please her mother and that she cares very much for Bingley. Clearly, he cares for her, as well. I will not stand in the way of love, and I will not assist you in doing so, either." He turned to Elizabeth. "I apologize for Miss Bingley's rudeness. Would you care to take a turn with me? I believe Bingley mentioned it earlier. We should try to pry him away from your mother so he and Miss Bennet can have a few moments alone."

Elizabeth continued to glare at Caroline as she nodded at Darcy. "Thank you, sir. I would be delighted to accompany you. May I add, thank you for defending my sister, who sees only the good in everyone and who thinks of certain people as friends who clearly are not." She felt a wave of satisfaction fill her when Caroline looked away first.

Chapter 5

Darcy, Bingley, Elizabeth, and Jane slowly began a second loop around the path. Mary, with a book under her nose, sat on a bench in the center of the garden and the youngest two girls pushed each other on the swing attached to a tall tree nearby. Suddenly, Lydia called out to her sisters.

"Charlotte has come, and has brought Stephen!" Lydia and Kitty ran to greet their friends.

When the two couples reached the driveway, they greeted the Lucas siblings with curtseys and bows. The group went into the house.

Though Caroline insisted the visit of the Bingley party had already extended beyond what was polite, they were encouraged to stay a bit longer for a piece of cake. Soon, however, Caroline and Louisa dropped enough hints to their brother that he reluctantly agreed to allow them to leave.

"Send the carriage back for me and Darcy, and do not delay." Bingley turned to his brother-in-law. "Hurst, see that they send it back immediately."

Hurst promised he would. "I will not allow either of them to countermand your orders to the coachman."

Jane and Bingley escorted his sisters and brother out, with Elizabeth and Darcy following. Caroline and the Hursts walked ahead of them all and entered the carriage, Caroline with false smiles and happy words for Jane, and nothing at all for her sister. Elizabeth watched the other woman ascend into the carriage with narrowed eyes.

Darcy laid his hand upon hers where it rested on his arm. "Do not allow Miss Bingley to get under your skin." He glanced at the equipage, shaking his head. "I used to find her amusing, but I confess I no longer do. She is accustomed to manipulating her brother to get what she wants, and he is no longer interested in allowing it." He nodded to where Bingley stood, giving instructions to his driver. "His care for your sister has gone a long way toward giving him the backbone to stand up to Caroline. Miss Bennet might just be the making of my friend." His lips lifted in the small smile he so often used.

"I am trying to rein in my anger, but I admit to being furious. Who does she think she is to speak of my sister so meanly, and in front of me?" Elizabeth shook her head. "I am sorry if I appear at a disadvantage, but such things bring out the protective nature in me. If I were a gentleman, I would ... I would darken her daylights."

Darcy chuckled. "I have no doubt you would." He pulled his head back a bit to look at her. "You are loyal to those you love."

Elizabeth glanced up at him before returning her gaze to the carriage to glare at it, as though she could burn a hole through it and the occupant. "I am. Blindly so, I have been told."

Darcy rubbed his fingers over her knuckles, drawing Elizabeth's attention back to him. "Perhaps one day, you will honor another with your loyalty." He lifted her hand, kissing the back.

Elizabeth was struck dumb by the feel of Darcy's lips as they barely brushed her appendage. She held it to her chest as she stared unblinkingly at the departing conveyance.

<center>~~~***~~~</center>

Inside the carriage, Caroline fumed. She had noted the way Darcy's eyes were drawn to Elizabeth from the moment he entered the room. She was flabbergasted when he went straight to the Bennet girl's side upon being invited to sit. Then, as she watched them interact, she felt rage rise in her breast. *So he likes her, does he? Clearly, he needs reminded of her poor origins and lack of fortune. So does my brother, the insensitive clod. Neither of them will go far in their infatuations with the Bennet fortune-hunters. Mark my words!*

When the equipage began to move and Bingley and Darcy waved, Caroline turned her head away. She could not speak calmly at the moment, and she knew she needed to be level-headed to get through to the two gentlemen. She decided she would take time to relax, perhaps in a hot bath, and prepare a list of arguments to present to them. *The first item on that list is going to be a reminder of the Bennets' lack of fortune,* she thought.

Caroline did exactly what she planned. As soon as she arrived at Netherfield and was handed down from the carriage, she charged into the house and up the stairs. She ordered bathwater from the housekeeper, Mrs. Nichols. Then, when she arrived in her dressing room before her maid could reach it from the kitchens, she berated the girl until the maid was almost in tears.

The next morning, Caroline arose with a plan in mind. She had spent a great deal of time, in the bath and out, creating her arguments and practicing their delivery. She felt confident that she would be able to sway Darcy from forming an attachment to Elizabeth Bennet, which would lead to her brother abandoning Jane, too.

Caroline chose her gown with care. It was important that she project what she was – a gentlewoman from a well-respected family who was educated in the best school for girls and who understood what it meant to be the wife of a member of high society. To appear in any other way would diminish her arguments, making them less effective than she needed them to be. She stood in front of the cheval mirror, turning this way and that, making sure she was as elegantly dressed as possible and appeared to best advantage. She dismissed her maid with a flick of her wrist. When she was alone, she smoothed her hands down the front of the day dress and took a deep breath. Then, she turned to the door and glided into the hall and down the stairs, her posture erect and spine stiff.

Caroline found Darcy and her brothers and sister in the small breakfast nook off the dining room. Immediately, she began to speak, not caring that she had interrupted her brother's conversation with his guest.

"Good! Everyone is here. We have need of a serious discussion." Caroline snatched a plate off the sideboard, tossed a scone on it, and moved to the table. Setting the plate down, she waited for the footman to seat her.

Bingley's brow quirked up. "A discussion about what?"

Without waiting to dismiss the servants, Caroline began. "About your choices, and about the unsuitability of the Bennet chits as wives."

Bingley gestured to the footmen to leave. Once the door had shut behind them, he glared at his sister. "What is unsuitable is your decision to discuss my business in front of the servants. You know they gossip."

Caroline sniffed. "They are unimportant. I am certain they do not understand above half of what I say. It is almost as if they speak a different language."

Bingley rolled his eyes as his elder sister gasped.

Darcy blotted his lips and stood. "I will meet you in the billiards room later, Bingley."

"Oh no, Mr. Darcy. This conversation involves you, as well. You must stay." Caroline gestured to his chair. "Do sit down."

With a crease between his brows and a glance at his friend, Darcy obliged her. He opened his mouth to inquire as to how a discussion about Bingley could have anything to do with him, but Caroline's voice cut him off.

"You cannot be serious, asking Miss Bennet for a courtship. You cannot marry her, and you will cause talk when you move on."

"Who says I cannot marry her?" Bingley sat back in his chair, crossing his arms over his chest.

"I say you cannot." Caroline gestured to Louisa. "We say you cannot. Papa would turn over in his grave at the thought of you marrying so far beneath you."

"Just how do you figure she is beneath me?" Bingley's jaw clenched. "She is a gentlewoman, born and bred. We are the children of a tradesman. A very successful and well-respected tradesman, but a tradesman nonetheless. Papa would be overjoyed that I have found a gentlewoman to love and who loves me in return."

"Pah." Caroline scoffed at Bingley's words. "Love has nothing to do with it. She is poor, Charles. She has no dowry."

"She has one thousand pounds upon her mother's death. I know this because Mr. Bennet and I discussed it. I have no need of a large dowry, and unless the factories suddenly stop producing, I have ample funds to care for any children we might have."

Caroline's eyes widened as she was temporarily distracted from the topic at hand. "What do you mean? I thought you were going to sell the factories?"

Bingley shrugged. "I had considered it, and I may still sell the two less valuable ones. However, I have recently become convinced that one can be a landed gentleman and still derive part of one's income from trade." He nodded toward Darcy. "Times are changing, and trade has not the stigma it once did."

"It does in the highest circles!" Caroline's horrified cry caused even Mr. Hurst to turn his eyes toward her.

"Well, no." Darcy cleared his throat. "Many of the peers in my uncle's circle are looking at the daughters of tradesmen to take to wife. Their estates are destitute, or nearly so, and the wealthier tradesmen dower their daughters very well." He shrugged. "As Bingley said, times are changing. Even those in the highest circles of society are seeing that the land will not sustain us forever. When Napoleon is defeated, the countries he has destroyed will begin growing their own crops again, and ours will not be needed. Forward-thinking gentlemen see this coming and adjust."

Caroline glowered at Darcy. "I have never heard of this before. I think you are making it up." She sniffed. "Regardless, my brother cannot marry Miss Bennet and you, Mr. Darcy, cannot court her sister. Even if we disregard their negligible dowry, their mother is an absolute horror, their younger sisters are unchecked, and their father exerts no control over any of them whatsoever. If either of you marry into that family, your own relatives will become laughingstocks. We will never be able to show our faces in society again." She shivered delicately. "They are grasping, social climbing fortune hunters. We have given our ball. We must now make haste to return to town, where there are plenty of appropriate young ladies to turn your heads."

"They are not fortune hunters!" Bingley banged his fist on the table and stood.

"Your brother is correct." Darcy glared at Caroline before turning to address the Hursts. "Before the ball began, I was coming out of the gentlemen's retiring room when I heard Miss Bennet's voice. She was talking to her sister, and I confess that once I realized Bingley was the topic of their conversation, I stopped to listen. Miss Bennet assured her sister that she cares greatly for Bingley and reminded Miss Elizabeth that she had vowed to marry for love, no matter what their mother's wishes were." Darcy turned to his friend, who was slowly sitting back down with a pleased smile growing across his face. "This is why I did not try to deter you from speaking to her. You know I was concerned."

Bingley nodded. "You were. You cautioned me to be certain of her regard and mine before I proceeded."

"I did. However, the conversation I overheard set my mind at ease. It is clear now that Miss Bennet adores you. I am happy you ignored my advice." Darcy grinned at his friend when Bingley laughed.

"She is an angel. Thank you, Darcy. You are the best of friends. I doubt I could find one better."

"But that mother!" Caroline felt desperation grow in her breast. "She is ridiculous, and if you married Miss Bennet, she would be here all the time and we," Caroline gestured between herself and Louisa, "would be forced to deal with her every day."

Bingley shrugged, his voice turning cool. "Who is to say I would make Netherfield my permanent home? It is just a lease, after all. I could give it up at any time, if I find something better. Besides, you will marry one day and have another gentleman's life to run. You will not be here forever."

Caroline glanced at Darcy and then back to her brother. "But –"

"No, Caroline, Darcy will not marry you. If he asked, I would not grant permission. He deserves someone who loves him for more than his position in life and his money. If he has found that person with Miss Elizabeth, I will encourage him." Bingley stopped speaking, as though something had popped into his brain and startled him. He leaned toward Caroline and shook his finger at her. "Even if you compromised him and were found nude in his bed, I would not allow him to marry you. You would be ruined and doomed to a life alone, so you think long and hard about something like that before you attempt it." Bingley stood again, this time tossing his napkin on his plate. "Louisa, Hurst, do you have anything to add to this discussion?"

Hurst shook his head as he swallowed. "Nothing beyond congratulations to you for standing up for yourself against your sister's wishes." He looked at his wife. "We will not stand in your way, will we, Louisa?"

Mrs. Hurst's eyes grew large as they darted between her husband, her brother, and the sister who was so good at forcing her to do things. She swallowed. "N-, no." She looked back at the fuming Caroline, wincing at the hard look on her sister's face, but then focused on her husband. "No, Reginald, we will not."

Hurst nodded once. "Good. I am glad to hear it. Bingley, feel free to carry on. As long as I have my sport, a comfortable place to nap, an occasional ragout, and the favors of my charming and lovely wife, I am a happy man. Best of luck to you in your courtship." He stood. "Same to you, Darcy." He bowed to the gentlemen and Caroline, then held his hand out to Louisa. "Come, Wife." When she tucked her hand in his and stood, he wrapped it around his elbow and escorted her out of the room.

Bingley looked down at his sister, triumph in his eyes. "Well, then. It seems you are out-numbered."

Caroline gritted her teeth as her eyes narrowed. She stood, jaw clenched, and tried to stare her brother down. She quickly real-ized he would not be intimidated. "Enjoy your victory while it lasts. You may have won the battle, but the war is not over." She wrenched her gaze away and turned, striding with sharp steps out the door and up the stairs.

Bingley blew out a breath. "I am sorry for that, Darcy. You did not deserve to be subjected to her and her ridiculous ideas."

"No apology is necessary." Darcy glanced toward the door. "Hopefully, she will not attempt to interfere further."

"I hope not, but I do not trust her. Caroline never gives up a fight easily." Bingley shook himself. "Enough of that. I am for Longbourn; do you care to accompany me?"

Darcy's lips lifted in a slow smile. "Indeed, I do. Thank you for asking."

Bingley laughed. "If I did not know better, I would say you must be in love." He cocked his head as he looked at his friend, whose small smile remained but who otherwise appeared inscrutable. "Are you?"

Darcy remained silent for a long moment before shrugging. "I could tell you, but then I would have to kill you." He laughed at the shocked look that accompanied Bingley's gasp. "Blame the colonel for that one." He came around the table, slapping his friend on the shoulder. "Are you coming?"

Bingley laughed and hurried after Darcy. "Your cousin is a regular out and outer, is he not?"

"He is." Darcy spoke over his shoulder as he walked down the hall toward the front door. "But, he has his uses." He winked, grinning briefly when Bingley laughed.

A quarter hour later, Darcy and Bingley were admitted to Longbourn.

Chapter 6

That evening, Darcy and Bingley returned late, having accepted an invitation from Mrs. Bennet to dine with the family. They entered the house in quiet conversation, having spent a pleasant afternoon with their lady loves. Having been informed by the housekeeper that Caroline and the Hursts were in the family parlor at the back of the house and would be pleased for the gentlemen to join them, they looked at each other and sighed.

"I suppose we must go in." Bingley hung his head. "I confess I would rather not."

"I feel the same, but it would be terribly rude to ignore them, and they are your family." Darcy looked down the hall, seeing light spill out from the room to illuminate the floor.

Bingley rolled his eyes. "Well, let us go in, then. Best get the unpleasantness over with right away."

Darcy shook his head but followed his friend to the parlor.

The gentlemen bowed when they entered. "I hope you all had as fine an afternoon as we did." Bingley stepped to his left to the cabinet that held carafes of port and sherry. "Darcy, can I get you something to drink?"

"A glass of port would be good, thank you." Darcy made his way to a wingback chair situated in front of a window but close to the seating area occupied by Caroline and her sister.

Caroline sniffed as she and Louisa sat down. "A fine afternoon. Ha! How could we, knowing what you were up to?"

"Caroline ..." Louisa's soft rebuke was ignored by her sibling.

"Do not start, Sister." Bingley handed Darcy his drink before taking up a place in a chair situated such that he could see both his friend and each of his family members. "Miss Bennet and Miss Elizabeth are both delightful young women. Darcy and I enjoyed ourselves very much."

"How you could enjoy yourself with such insipid creatures is beyond me, frankly." Caroline's sharp words quieted the entire room. "Miss Bennet is mealy-mouthed, and from what I understand, her sister is a blue-stocking. Neither is wife material, not for a gentleman of good standing."

Bingley could see Darcy stiffening and attempted to diffuse the situation. "Caroline, if you cannot keep a civil tongue in your head, I will take action. Mark my words."

Caroline sneered. "What could you do? I will say what I wish to in my own home."

Bingley leaned forward, and though he lowered his voice, everyone could hear his words. "What I can do is cut off your allowance.

Perhaps a few weeks without the ability to shop will curb your tongue." He leaned back.

As Caroline sputtered in shock, Hurst spoke. "I am happy to hear you had such a pleasant evening. Both those girls are lovely, inside and out."

"They are." Bingley grinned, happy that his brother had diverted the conversation. I think Miss Elizabeth will be good for Darcy. She challenged him at every turn this evening. I think she beat him at chess, too." He laughed to see Darcy grin.

"Oh, ho!" Hurst chuckled. "I have seen Darcy play chess. He is an excellent strategist. Did he allow her to win, or did she do it on her own merit?"

"I did not allow her to win. She has the sharpest mind of any female I have ever met, and that includes my Aunt Audra." Darcy laughed. "I did underestimate her skills, however. Her father gleefully pointed that out to me."

"And, Darcy took it all in stride." Bingley shook his head. "From where Miss Bennet and I were sitting, it appeared that Miss Elizabeth was just as competitive as you ever were, my friend. I asked Jane about it, and she confirmed that her sister hates to lose."

Hurst laughed. "There it is, proof they are a perfect match."

Darcy blushed but his grin widened. "I believe you are correct, Hurst."

Bingley was the only gentleman who noticed Caroline angrily standing and hastening out of the room, her skirts swishing. He shrugged it off. Louisa bit her lip to see it, but remained at her husband's side.

~~~***~~~

The remaining group stayed belowstairs for a quarter hour before retiring for the night. Darcy's thoughts were full of Elizabeth as he allowed his valet to assist him in preparing for bed. Eventually, he was changed from his regular clothing to his nightshirt. He seated himself at the desk in his room, his journal in front of him and a glass of port at his elbow. He smiled to himself as he filled two pages and half a third with his account of the evening spent with the young woman who had captured his attention and heart.

Finished with the journal entry, he closed the book, capped the ink bottle, and set his pen down in the tray. Picking up his port, he leaned back, smiling at the memory of Elizabeth's triumphant crowing when she captured his queen at the conclusion of their game of chess.

"I have never felt such a pull towards a woman before." Darcy held up his glass, looking at the liquid inside with its glow from the fire behind it. "It is as though I have come home after a long journey." Taking a sip of port, he felt its warmth spread through his in-
~~~

sides. He smiled for a moment, but then caught his lower lip between his teeth. "It is so soon; we have known each other mere days. My relatives will question me on that." He lapsed into thought, considering the probable arguments his aunts, uncles, and cousins would use. His sister he did not worry about. She trusted him and would accept his choice, if he followed his inclination to pursue Elizabeth.

After another half hour of arguing in his mind, Darcy tossed off the last of the liquid in the glass, placed it on the table, blew out the candles, and climbed into bed. He reclined, his hands under his head, and sighed. "I will simply have to remind them all of my father's reaction to my mother. The Darcy side of the family, at least, will accept her, then." With those words echoing in his dark chamber, he drifted off to sleep.

The next day, Darcy and Bingley again visited Longbourn. As had happened the day before, Netherfield's female occupants and Mr. Hurst remained at home. The weather was pleasant, so the gentlemen invited the Bennet ladies to take a turn in the garden.

"Tell me more about your family." Elizabeth tilted her head up to give Darcy an arch smile. "You have told me about your uncle the earl, but very little about the rest of your relatives."

"The countess is much like you. She is intelligent and well-read and challenges her husband at every turn. Lord Matlock and his sons often tell her *she* should have been the politician." Darcy chuckled. "She is of great use to my uncle; she speaks on his behalf to the wives of his peers in the House of Lords, who, she says, have great influence on their husbands."

Elizabeth covered a giggle with her hand. "It has been my observation that your aunt is correct. My mother is certainly a very big influence on my father."

Darcy shook his head. "That was not well done of you, forcing me to comment on your parents that way."

Elizabeth laughed. "It was not, was it? I apologize. You may feel free to ignore my statement and change the subject."

Darcy flashed a grin at his companion. "Thank you." He cleared his throat. "Back to my relatives, the earl and countess have two sons. The viscount is thirty and courting the sister of one of his friends. The younger of my cousins is a colonel in the Horse Guards. He is a year older than I and is the gentleman who shares guardianship of my sister with me."

"Ah, a soldier." Elizabeth nodded. "My youngest sisters would be happy to meet him." She grinned.

Darcy groaned. "Lovely. I shall have to warn him to steer clear."

"Why, Mr. Darcy, one would think you dislike my sisters!" Elizabeth placed her hand over her heart and affected a look of horror.

With another shake of his head, Darcy rolled his eyes. He could not prevent a wide smile from spreading over his features. Then, he sobered as he explained the last of his relatives. "I have one more aunt on my mother's side, Lady Catherine de Bourgh. She is much like the earl in manner: authoritative and demanding." He sighed. "She has a daughter who she insists I am engaged to, by way of my mother and herself arranging it when Anne and I were babes. My father roundly denied it, and Mother never mentioned it to me when she was still alive."

Elizabeth's eyes had gone wide. "So ... you are not, in fact, engaged to this cousin?"

Darcy rushed to reassure her. "I am not. I never have been and never will be. My cousin and I have discussed it at length since we reached adulthood and are agreed that we would not suit." He shrugged. "We allow Lady Catherine to have her say because it has, to now, not hurt anyone to do so. She will not hear what she does not wish to, so we would be wasting our effort, in any case."

Elizabeth blew out a breath she had been holding. "Good." She jumped a bit and clapped her hand over her mouth before peeking up to see Darcy's expression.

Pleased to hear Elizabeth's opinion, Darcy grinned for a moment. The warm feeling that filled him to hear of her regard faded as another reality intruded upon him. "Lady Catherine has made noises over the years since my father's passing about gaining custody of my sister. She has increased the pressure since the summer, when Georgiana's trip to Ramsgate had an unfortunate conclusion. My sister is only fifteen years old and is terrified of the idea of living with our aunt, who, to be frank, is a bit of a harridan."

"I am sorry. The courts will not grant such a request, though, will they? Does custody of minors not always go to a male relative?"

Darcy shrugged. "It would be difficult, though not impossible. The earl and countess, if they could be swayed to her point of view, could testify on her behalf. They have remained firmly on my side so far. That is in my favor."

"Do you fear they might change their minds?" Elizabeth could not look at Darcy, because they were skirting a wet spot in the path and she had to watch where her feet landed.

"As long as Georgiana remains with them, or with me and I stay in town, no. However, if I were to allow her to go on holiday again, they might change their minds. I doubt my sister would repeat her behavior, but she is full young. One can never tell what goes on in the mind of a young lady." Darcy's mien had transformed, all humor wiped away.

Elizabeth was silent for a moment before she replied. "You have not given me the details of your sister's mishap," she began in a soft voice, "but as the sister to a fifteen year old, I can fully agree that a person cannot begin to fathom what happens in their brains." She cleared her throat. "I do not see you as anything but a responsible gentleman, and I hope you do not feel guilty for whatever it is that happened. Your sister is clearly among the living and, from what I gather, in good health. Therefore, you have done your duty to her very well. I choose to believe that your aunt and uncle will continue to support you, as will I, for all the good it will do you."

Darcy stopped, turning toward Elizabeth. He gazed upon her for a long moment, his heart full to the brim with love. "Thank you, Miss Elizabeth. You are kindness itself. Your support means the world to me." He felt the urge to lean forward and brush her lips with his, but stiffened his spine against it. It was too soon, and they were not engaged. *Soon,* he thought. *Soon, I will propose. In the meantime ...* "You have not asked, but I would imagine you are curious about the event?"

Startled, Elizabeth replied with caution. "I confess I am; however, if you do not wish to tell me, you do not have to. Nothing you could say would make me abandon our friendship."

With a small smile and another squeeze of Elizabeth's hands, Darcy began to tell the tale. "I removed Georgiana from school this past spring and formed an establishment for her under the supervision of a companion, Mrs. Younge." Darcy tucked Elizabeth's hand under his arm once more and resumed their walk. "It turns out that my cousin and I were deceived as to the woman's character. She had a connection to a man known to me, who I had grown up with but whose character had led to a break between us."

Darcy paused in his speech to press Elizabeth's fingers under his own when she squeezed his arm. "Mrs. Younge convinced me to approve a trip to Ramsgate over the summer for her and Georgiana. There, the companion allowed him, my former friend, to call on my sister, whose only memories of him were that of a young child. Between them, they soon convinced my sister to elope with him and to surprise me with the news later." He swallowed and looked down. When he spoke next, his voice cracked. "It was only my unexpected visit that stopped them. Seeing me in person, Georgiana could not keep the news to herself."

Elizabeth's free hand rose to cover her mouth, horror having made it drop open. "Oh, no! The poor girl! What happened then?"

"I immediately sent a note to the man's lodgings, demanding he leave the city and never contact me or my sister again. Georgiana was heartbroken when he left without a word to her."

Elizabeth's eyes filled with tears. She dropped her hand from her mouth to cover his fingers where they lay on top of hers. "I am sorry, for both of you. What was the man's reason for attempting such a thing?"

"Undoubtedly, my sister's dowry. At thirty thousand pounds, it makes her a target for all manner of unscrupulous men, or will when she is out." Darcy's mien took on the angry edge she had seen before. "I have no doubt he also wished revenge on me."

"Revenge?" Elizabeth shook her head. "But, why?"

"My father left him one thousand pounds and a living in his will, if the man should take orders." Darcy glanced at Elizabeth. "Father had sent him to Cambridge along with me, and paid for his education. I had first-hand knowledge of this man's behavior and knew him to be unsuited to the church. When ..." He paused and then began again. "When the man came to me after Father's will was probated and I was declared the owner of the estate, he was displeased with his inheritance. He asked for a sum of money to replace the living and said he wanted to study law. After some negotiation, he accepted a sum of three thousand pounds."

"So, he left you with ..." Elizabeth added the numbers in her head. "Four thousand pounds! What did he need your sister's dowry for?"

Chuckling darkly, Darcy replied. "He had run through that four thousand pounds in two years. He needed money to live on."

Elizabeth's eyes grew wide. "A person could live for decades on four thousand pounds!"

"Yes, this is true." Darcy nodded.

"Well." Elizabeth shook her head again and pulled her gaze from Darcy's. "I am happy you saved your sister from him. She would have had a miserable life and been left destitute. Is she much recovered?"

"She is better, yes. My aunt tells me she has some lingering feelings of guilt and is probably forever changed, but she is no longer distraught."

"Good." Elizabeth spoke softly. "She will find love one day. True love." She looked up at Darcy with a soft expression in her eyes.

Darcy gazed into Elizabeth's orbs and felt like he was falling. His feet stopped moving just long enough for him to reply. "As have others before her."

Chapter 7

That evening, Darcy and Bingley returned from Longbourn earlier than they had the day before. Though they had received another invitation from Mrs. Bennet to dine with her, Bingley had felt obliged to eat with his family, and Darcy had concurred. There was no point in antagonizing Miss Bingley more than they had to.

When they entered the house, they could hear Caroline speaking in the drawing room at the front of the building. As they handed their things to the waiting housekeeper, they listened in silence.

"I cannot believe our brother is being so stubborn about this! And you, Louisa, allowing that oaf you married to force you to support him. What were you thinking?"

Louisa's voice was softer, but still clear. "I was thinking he was my husband. I was also thinking how nice it would be to not be forced to dominate Charles for once, and allow him to be his own man."

Caroline scoffed. "Forced. Good heavens, anyone would think you believed our brother capable of making good choices on his own."

"Have we ever given him the opportunity to do so? Have we not, every single time he had to make a decision, persuaded him to do what *you* wished, instead of what *he* wanted?"

"What is this emphasis on my wishes? You took part." Caroline's voice sounded further away.

"You know very well that most of the time you pushed and prodded me and would not leave me be until I supported you." Louisa's voice took on an edge of anger. "Do not stand there now and deny it. You, Sister, are a bully and always have been. Your methods may have become more refined, but they still exist. Reginald is correct: we must allow Charles to make his own decisions. He is an educated adult. He has made excellent connections and is intelligent and shrewd. If he is in love with Miss Bennet, who are we to try to persuade him otherwise?"

"Love! Why does everyone speak of love? Love is meaningless in this world. We need our brother to marry above us. Way above us." There was a pause. "Unless Mr. Darcy can be persuaded to marry me."

"Charles would not allow that. He told you this."

"I think Mr. Darcy could be persuaded, though. He must be made to see that Eliza Bennet is not worthy of his regard. The same for Jane Bennet with Charles. I must make both of them see the Bennets for what they truly are: poor, worthless, and grasping. With a mother like theirs, they will surely mature into terrors. How can they not? Eliza is well on her way already, with her conceited independence and wild manner."

"Caroline ..."

"No, listen, Louisa! It is all true, and our brother and his friend must be convinced it is so. We must find a way to prove it to them."

Darcy and Bingley had continued to listen to Caroline's ravings with growing anger. When Hurst descended the stairs to join them, they decided without words to end her ranting. They stepped into the drawing room to witness Louisa stand with a white face while her sister paced away, still speaking ill of the Bennets.

"Caroline Beatrice Bingley, you will cease speaking of the woman I love in such a manner right now." Bingley, countenance flushed a deep red, stalked after his sister, who had whirled, eyes wide, when she heard his voice.

"Charles!" Caroline's hand fluttered up to her neck. "I did not hear you enter."

"Clearly." Charles spoke through gritted teeth, veins popping out in his neck. "Do you remember what I told you last evening?"

Caroline's eyes darted around the room, looking everywhere but at her brother. "I-, I d-do not."

Charles ground his teeth as his eyes narrowed. "I warned you that I will suspend your pin money if you do not cease speaking derogatively of Miss Bennet and her family. This is your final warning. Heed it well."

Caroline gulped. Without a word, she curtseyed to him and left the room.

Charles whirled toward Louisa, who instantly cried out, "I defended you!"

"I heard you." He swallowed, looking away and shaking his shoulders out. "Thank you."

"You are welcome." Louisa glanced at Hurst, who nodded. "I apologize to you for allowing her to bully me into swaying you to her point of view all these years. It was wrong of me, and I am sorry."

"I forgive you." Bingley glanced at his brother-in-law and then looked back at his sister. "You will not do it again?"

"Only if I truly believe you will be harmed. Even then, I will state my opinion and trust you to make the decision you think is best. I will not berate you, nor will I nag you about it." Louisa looked at Hurst again, taking the hand he held out to her. "My husband has convinced me of the error of my ways. I let him down, as well, and am making amends. I am grateful he stood up to Caroline yesterday. That action seems to have snapped us out of our stalemate."

Hurst lifted his wife's hand and kissed the back of it. "It was past time I did. Seeing your brother take charge for once gave me the push I needed to follow suit." He winked at Charles. "See how one action on the part of one person can effect changes in everyone around him?"

Charles shook his head and laughed. "I never would have thought ..." He turned to Darcy. "Would you?"

"Not in a million years." Darcy strode forward to shake Hurst's hand. "Good on you, Hurst." He turned to Bingley, slapping his friend on the shoulder. "And, good on you, Bingley. It is about time."

The bell rang to announce the meal. Bingley and Darcy looked at each other and shrugged.

"I suppose it is too late to change before dinner now." Bingley looked at Louisa. "Do you mind two dusty gentlemen at the table with you?"

Louisa smiled, her hand tucked into the crook of Hurst's arm. "I do not mind at all, as long as it is not an everyday occurrence."

"We promise." Bingley leaned over and kissed her cheek before stepping back to allow the couple to lead them to the dining room.

After the meal, which was eaten without Caroline present because she had requested a tray in her rooms, Darcy and Bingley popped up the stairs for a quick wash and a change of clothes before rejoining the Hursts in the drawing room. There, they were presented with the day's post, which had been given to Louisa earlier in the evening.

Darcy received several letters. He sorted through them as he wandered across the room to a chair. Two were from his steward at Pemberley, three from stewards at lesser estates that he owned, one was from the earl, one was in Lady Catherine's handwriting, and one was from his sister. Darcy chose that one to open first. He missed Georgiana and was eager to discover how she was faring. He scanned the note quickly, then settled in for a longer, more serious perusal of the contents.

> *Dear Brother,*
>
> *All is well here in London. The weather has been difficult, but at least it is not snowing yet.*
>
> *Aunt Audra and Uncle Henry took me to the Menagerie the other day. I was fascinated by all the animals on display. It is a shame that so many visitors had to torment the poor things. My aunt said that is just the way of life, that the world is full of circumstances that are difficult and that I must harden myself to it. I did not argue with her, but I have to wonder why it must be so. Can we not change that? Become softer, more gentle people?*
>
> *Thank you for your vivid descriptions of Netherfield and of Miss Elizabeth and her family. I felt almost as though I were there with you. Do you like Miss E. very much, then? It seems as though you*

do. From your descriptions, I think I would like her, even if you do not.

May I make a request? I wish for you to be happy, Brother. You above everyone I know deserves it. You have put up with so much as my guardian. If you do like Miss E., if she makes you happy and loves you completely, will you bring her home to me as my sister?

Before I go, I must mention that I have received another letter from my Aunt Catherine. It was filled with admonishments about practicing the pianoforte and my languages, and disparaged you rather fiercely for daring to be a gentleman and in charge of me. Her missive has rather frightened me. Aunt Audra was dismissive of it, but that was not reassuring.

I am eager to see you again. I love you.

G. Darcy

Darcy lowered the letter to his lap as he contemplated the words his sister had written. He could well imagine Lady Matlock shrugging and advising his sister to toughen up. *Rather like telling a leopard to change its spots,* he thought. Georgiana was the most tenderhearted soul he had ever known. She took after their mother that way.

Darcy read the last paragraph again, his temperature rising at Lady Catherine's hubris in writing words of that nature to such a sensitive girl. *Who does she think she is, going on that way to my sister? When I write my aunt next, I will tell her to stop corresponding with Georgiana if she cannot keep her opinions to herself. I will remind her that I am the head of my family. That should stop her mouth temporarily, at least. But, how to make it permanent?*

In the back of his mind, Darcy knew the answer. Elizabeth's face floated at the edge of his consciousness. *Yes,* he thought. *She will save us from this situation.* Darcy reread the portion of the letter that mentioned the woman he had fallen instantly in love with. *It will make Georgiana happy if I marry Elizabeth, and it will make me happy, as well.* He thought about the feeling of coming home that he experienced whenever he was in Elizabeth Bennet's presence, and the bolt of electricity that shot to his heart from whatever part of him that touched her. *Every single time,* he thought, his smile slowly growing. *I want that. I want it forever. I will propose the very next time I see her.*

<div align="center">~~~***~~~</div>

The next day, Darcy and Bingley visited Longbourn, this time with the Hursts. It was overcast and cold, so the party elected to remain within the house. They broke up into small groups in the drawing room to chat and play games.

Darcy drew Elizabeth to a chaise lounge on the far side of the room. Bingley and Jane were nearby but not close enough to hear anything. Mary was in the music room next door, practicing on the pianoforte. Lydia and Kitty were playing cards by one window, and Mrs. Bennet had Louisa and Hurst at the other, discussing last week's ball.

"You appear to have something on your mind, sir." Elizabeth's brow arched.

"I do." Darcy glanced nervously around the room, then back at Elizabeth. "I have something to ask you."

Elizabeth's eyes widened. "You do?"

"Yes." Darcy inhaled deeply, his attention distracted by the lavender scent Elizabeth wore. He closed his eyes for just a second and savored the odor, but swiftly forced his mind back to the task at hand. "Miss Elizabeth, when I first saw you, I was struck by the expression in your beautiful eyes, and by your elegance and grace." He itched to hold her hand but refrained. "The longer I spend time with you, the more impressed I am with your other qualities. You are kind and gentle, intelligent, and competitive, not to mention fiercely loyal to the ones you love." He swallowed, curling his hands into fists after catching himself wiping the palms on his breeches. "I have come to long for that loyalty, that love, to be bestowed on me. I love you, with all that I am. Will you marry me?"

Elizabeth covered her gaping mouth with her hand. She swallowed, tears flooding her eyes. "Thank you for the honor of your proposal, Mr. Darcy. I have fallen in love with you, as well, and I would be happy to marry you."

Now Darcy gave in to the urge to hold Elizabeth's hand. He squeezed it, reaching his free hand up to wipe the tear that ran down her cheek. "Happy tears, I hope?"

"Oh, yes. Very happy, indeed." Elizabeth's bright but watery smile brought out an answering one of Darcy's.

"Good." Another squeeze to Elizabeth's small hand and Darcy stood. "I should go speak to your father."

"Yes. I will take you to him." Elizabeth rose, murmured an excuse to her mother and their guests, and led Darcy out of the room and to Mr. Bennet's book room.

Chapter 8

A quarter hour later, Mr. Bennet entered the drawing room, Elizabeth and Darcy behind him. Clearing his throat, he claimed the attention of the room's occupants.

"Mrs. Bennet, I have news."

"Well, what is it? I am entertaining; I do not have all day."

Bennet's right brow rose but he ignored his wife's impertinence. "It seems one of your daughters has accepted a proposal today."

Mrs. Bennet's eyes widened and she shot a look toward Jane and Bingley, who sat waiting, one serenely and one with a large smile on his face. The matron's brow creased. "Jane?"

"It is not, in fact, your eldest daughter who will be marrying. At least, not that I know of." Bennet sent a look toward Bingley, half glare and half sarcasm.

"Not Jane?" Mrs. Bennet looked around at her younger girls before realizing that Elizabeth stood near her father instead of being seated on the far wall, and that Mr. Darcy was standing with her. "Lizzy?"

"Indeed, your second child has accepted Mr. Darcy's hand in marriage. The pair of them wish to marry soon, probably before

Christmas. You are experienced in pulling off dinners quickly and with aplomb. Do you think you are up to the challenge of a wedding breakfast in, say, three weeks?"

"Three weeks?" Mrs. Bennet's shriek made everyone in the room cringe. "I cannot plan a wedding to a man of Mr. Darcy's stature in three weeks! Perhaps three months ..."

"No, Mama. We have reasons for wishing to marry soon, reasons that involve his sister and that we will not be discussing with you." Elizabeth knew she needed to be firm with her mother. "We have already discussed it with Papa, and he is in agreement with our timeline."

"But-"

"Mrs. Bennet, if I may interrupt ..." Darcy paused. "I believe my aunt and uncle, the Earl and Countess of Matlock, will be able to attend if Elizabeth and I marry on December twentieth. If we wait until spring, they may not be able to attend at all."

Mrs. Bennet's mouth made an O as the implications of hosting an earl and countess began to crowd out all other considerations. Finally, after several long minutes and with everyone in the room staring at her, she was able to reply. "You say their schedules will not accommodate a later wedding?" She peered up at Darcy, watching him closely.

"That is it, exactly. They would wish to see their only nephew marry, and to do that, we would have to have the ceremony no later than the twentieth of this month."

With a decisive nod of her head, the mistress of Longbourn consented. "Very well, then. It will be a challenge, I grant you, but for an earl and a countess, all things are possible." She turned away to return to her seat. "Just think how jealous Lady Lucas will be!" She giggled, then began to question Louisa about weddings she had attended in town.

Bennet rolled his eyes with a wry grin. "Well, there you have it, Lizzy. Permission to marry on the date you chose. Congratulations." To Darcy, he added, "To you, as well, sir. Tomorrow when you visit, we can discuss the settlement in detail. Do you wish me to make arrangements for a common license, or would you prefer a special license?"

"A special license would require a trip to town. I would rather not be gone from Elizabeth that long if I did not have to." He smiled down at his betrothed, who still clung to his arm.

"I agree. A common license is enough. But do not allow Mama to hear us discuss it or she will force you to get the more expensive one." Elizabeth smirked.

"Very wise, Daughter." Bennet laughed. "We will stop speaking about it."

"I will talk to the rector, but thank you for offering." Darcy nodded to his future father-in-law. "And thank you for supporting our desire."

Bennet waved him off. "No need to thank me. I rather enjoy my wife's displays when she is distressed." He shrugged. "I hope to do it again when your friend comes to the point with my eldest, but if I know Jane, she will do whatever he mother wishes."

Elizabeth giggled. "She will. She always does. Jane is a peacemaker."

With a laugh, Bennet told his favorite daughter and her betrothed to join the rest of the party and retreated back to his book room and silence.

Though Darcy, Bingley, and the Hursts turned down Mrs. Bennet's invitation to dine, they remained at Longbourn long enough to accept a celebratory cup of tea and some cakes the cook had made that morning.

On the return trip to Netherfield, Darcy accepted the congratulations of his friends with cheer. It was decided among the four occupants of the carriage that Caroline be informed of the engagement in the morning. They all hoped for a pleasant dinner, and Darcy wished for his happiness to linger as long as possible before it was interrupted.

~~~***~~~

The next day, the gentlemen of Netherfield went hunting in the morning. They knew the Bennet ladies had planned a day of shopping and visiting the neighbors and would not
~~~

be available until late in the day. They had secured an invitation for the entire Netherfield party to dine at Longbourn that evening. Mrs. Bennet wished to begin the celebrations for her daughter's engagement with a dinner party in her own home.

By the time Darcy, Bingley, and Hurst returned to the house, got cleaned up and changed, and came back downstairs, Caroline and Louisa were breaking their fast.

"Ah, eggs and kippers. Nothing like a hearty meal to begin one's day." Hurst kissed his wife on the cheek, then went straight to the sideboard, where he piled a plate full of food.

"I heartily agree." Bingley loaded his own plate. He nudged Darcy, who stood beside him. When his friend looked his way, he tilted his head in a nod toward his sister. "Nothing like a good meal to prepare the stomach for a difficult task, eh, Darcy?"

"Indeed." Darcy finished making his selections and found a seat at the table as far from Caroline as he could get.

The group ate largely in silence, each lost in their own thoughts. Finally, Caroline and Louisa pushed their plates away and concentrated on their cups of tea. Darcy took note of this, looked at Bingley, who nodded to him, and then set his fork down on the edge of his plate.

"I have an announcement to make." Darcy waited for all eyes to turn towards him.

The Hursts and Bingley had agreed to behave as though news of Darcy's engagement was just that – news – and to pretend they did not already know of it. "Last evening, I asked Miss Elizabeth to marry me, and she accepted. We immediately sought her father's permission, which he instantly and happily granted. We are to be married on the twentieth of this month." Darcy's eyes had never left Caroline during this announcement, so he could clearly see her shock.

After a long moment of silence, Bingley and the Hursts broke out in applause, congratulating Darcy on his happy news. Caroline finally closed her mouth, which had fallen open as he had spoken. Her sharp voice rang out above the sound of her family's chatter.

"You cannot be serious. You have tied yourself to that unladylike, miserable little chit?"

"Caroline!" Bingley stood, tipping his chair back onto the floor.

His stare implacable, Darcy held Caroline's eyes. "I have, quite happily. Mrs. Bennet has invited all of us to dinner tonight to celebrate. It will be one of many parties we will attend to share our joy with the neighborhood."

Caroline stood, fists planted on the table. "Your joy." She sneered. "We shall see how long that joy lasts when you realize how little she really brings you." Ignoring her brother's shout and her sister's pleading, she turned and marched out the door.

Darcy, out of habit, had stood when Caroline did. Now, he sat back down and blew out a breath. "Well," he said, "that went very well, did it not?" He picked up his coffee and took a sip.

Bingley, who had made a move toward the door as if to follow his sister, stopped and turned. "You think so?"

Darcy shrugged. "She did not throw anything at my head and kept her comments short. It could have been worse."

Louisa giggled. "He is correct, Brother. Caroline usually breaks everything within reach when she is angry."

Bingley thought about that for a few seconds and then laughed. "I guess you are right." He returned to the table. "I did tell her that any further disparaging remarks would be met with the loss of her pin money, so I will have to write to my solicitor and send letters to all the shops."

"Better send it express." Hurst winked as he lifted his cup to his lips.

With the mood of the room restored, the four finished breaking their fasts and turned to their day's activities.

Finally, the hour arrived for the Netherfield party to make its way to Longbourn. All but Caroline gathered in the entry hall, waiting for the younger woman to come down. After a quarter hour, Louisa went up to see what was taking her sister so long. She came back down the stairs shaking her head.

"Caroline has developed a headache and has begged off. She says she will call for a tray when she wakes up, but she is going to try to sleep it off." Louisa paused. "She was rather cold to me, but she was not rude and did not try to make me take her part."

"That is good." Bingley patted his sister on the shoulder. "It will be far pleasanter without her, anyway. Come, let us go."

~~~***~~~

Caroline stood in the window of her bedchamber and watched the curve of the drive. From her vantage point, she would be able to see the carriage as it drove away but her family and Mr. Darcy would not be able to see her. Within minutes, the equipage crept past, the coachman urging the horses to go faster once they were on the straight part of the driveway. She watched as the conveyance grew smaller. When she could no longer see it, she whirled around and began pacing her bedroom.

"So, Mr. Darcy is engaged to Eliza Bennet, is he? Charles will soon follow suit with Jane, no doubt." Caroline spit the words out as her anger began to boil over. "I will not have it, not for either of them." She came to
~~~

the end of the clear space at one end of the chamber and spun on her heel to march the other direction. "I do not care what Louisa and her sop of a husband say, Charles is not capable of making his own decisions. I *thought* Darcy would be of help to him by leading him in the correct direction, but clearly I was wrong." She shook her head. "What a disappointment he has turned out to be." She stopped in her tracks at the other end of the room. "When he marries me, I will take care of everything. Men are easy enough to lead around. Charles has shown me that, and it is plain to see that Darcy and Charles are more alike than I had thought."

Caroline resumed her advance across the room. As she paced, options and plans began forming in her mind. "I will prevent Darcy and Charles from marrying into the Bennet family, and I ..." She stopped in front of the cheval glass. "I will be the next mistress of Pemberley. Mark my words!"

Chapter 9

At Longbourn, Darcy and Bingley were welcomed by the ladies with smiles and, on Mrs. Bennet's part, much fluttering of handkerchiefs. They bowed and smiled at the matron, but their eyes were on their beloveds and as soon as was practicable, the gentlemen planted themselves at their ladies' sides.

"How are you today, my dear?" Darcy helped Elizabeth sit after bowing to her and kissing her hand. He seated himself beside her, his gaze snared by the sight of her smiling lips. His own tingled in anticipation of kissing her. The only thing that stopped him, in the end, was a question from Mrs. Bennet.

"Elizabeth will tell me nothing of your favorite dishes, Mr. Darcy. I must make sure they are on the menu for the wedding breakfast; will you not tell me yourself?"

Darcy glanced at his betrothed, who was rolling her eyes. "Do not be upset with Elizabeth. We have not been in company enough that she would know my preferred dishes."

Mrs. Bennet harrumphed and cast a suspicious eye toward her second child. "I suppose you are right. Still, my question stands: what do you prefer I serve?"

"Anything is fine, madam. I do prefer beef to mutton and poultry or game birds above fish. I also enjoy well-cooked venison."

Mrs. Bennet gave Darcy a nod. "Thank you, sir. I will endeavor to keep mutton and fish to a minimum." She waved toward Elizabeth. "That was my only question for now. Please do give my daughter some attention, lest she blame me for keeping you away."

"Mama!" Elizabeth's cheeks turned scarlet.

"I was teasing, Lizzy." Mrs. Bennet shook her head. "Now go, keep that young man interested." She winked and turned back to the paper sitting on the table before her, writing something down on what appeared from a distance to be a list.

Elizabeth huffed and rolled her eyes. She turned to Darcy. "I am sorry."

Darcy's lips lifted as his eyes devoured her face. "Think nothing of it. She loves you, even if her habits and propensities make me cringe at times."

With a second roll of her eyes, Elizabeth changed the subject. "Are you to speak to Papa today about the settlement? He mentioned something about it this morning."

"I am, but I wish to spend some time with you before I meet with him." Darcy slid deeper into the couch, positioning himself at an angle so as to see his affianced more easily.

Elizabeth mirrored Darcy's position, tucking one leg under the other as she did so. "Good, for if I had my way, you would only spend time with me."

"I would rather that be the case, but until we are married, it cannot be." Darcy leaned forward, lowering his voice so that only Elizabeth could hear what he next said. "That is probably for the best, because were we to be alone for very long, I am uncertain I could refrain from kissing you senseless and then taking shocking liberties with your person."

Elizabeth blushed scarlet. For a long moment, she look horrified, but soon her wide eyes narrowed and her mouth closed. She looked Darcy up and down, slowly examining what she could see of him as a slow smile spread over her lips. "I see." With a wink, she turned her still-reddened countenance away briefly, looking back when he chuckled. "You, sir, are a tease."

Darcy shrugged one shoulder, a smirk twisting his lips. "Perhaps I am, but I am your tease."

Elizabeth grinned at that, a large, glowing smile that transformed her face. "I know, and it makes me very happy."

After some further banter, Darcy and Elizabeth rose, and she escorted him to her father's book room.

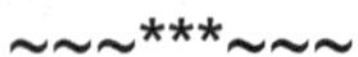

"Would you like to sit in on this discussion, Lizzy? You are as well-versed in accounting as anyone I have met. None of this will be a mystery to you, I should think. Is that acceptable to you, Mr. Darcy?" Bennet peered up at his future son-in-law from behind his desk.

"Perfectly so. I wish to begin this marriage as I intend it to go on, and that means that my concerns are Elizabeth's and hers are mine." Darcy turned to his betrothed. "If you wish to remain, my love, I would be happy to have you here."

Elizabeth looked fondly at Darcy. "Thank you, I believe I shall stay. It will ease my mind to know the details." She slid her favorite chair closer to Darcy's and seated herself.

A half hour later, the discussion finished with a draft document being written up by Darcy, who would send it express to his solicitor in London.

~~~***~~~

Two days later, another dinner was planned, this one at Lucas Lodge. Elizabeth and Jane were doing each other's hair as they prepared for the event, to save Longbourn's one upper house maid some running back and forth. Elizabeth was currently in the chair, and Jane was pinning one of several braids to her sister's head. Elizabeth sat as still as she could, watching the movement of a
~~~

tiny silk rosebud attached to the end of a hairpin as she spun it.

"I wonder if Miss Bingley will be prevailed upon to attend tonight. She has yet to extend her congratulations." Elizabeth glanced up at Jane in the mirror, her left brow rising above a downturned lip.

"Mr. Bingley has said she will, if he has to tie her up to get her there. He told me he has cut off her pin money because she was so rude about your engagement." Jane spoke around the pins in her mouth. Her focus remained on her sister's hair.

Elizabeth's right brow joined her left. "He did?" She blinked. "That seems a rather harsh punishment. She must have said some shocking things."

"Mr. Bingley indicated that it had been an ongoing problem." Jane paused, one braid finally placed to her satisfaction, and pulled the remaining pins out of her mouth. She looked into the mirror and Elizabeth's eyes. "She is unhappy about our courtship, as well, but Mr. Bingley insists she will not come between us. He said his sister is in the habit of manipulating him, and that Mrs. Hurst has gone along with it, until now." She shrugged. "I told him I do not wish to come between him and his family, and that surely Miss Bingley means well, but he insisted she does not and that if he allows her, he will end up married to *her* choice of a wife instead of me, for whom he cares." She popped the pins back into her mouth and began to carefully arrange another braid into a circle.

"It sounds as though he plans to propose soon." Elizabeth teased her elder sister. "Perhaps, if he ever does, we might have a double wedding." She laughed to see Jane's reflection roll her eyes. "I am sorry to be the cause of trouble in the Bingley family, but not sorry enough to give up Mr. Darcy." She sobered. "I suspect we will have enough trouble with certain of his family members. We do not need your Mr. Bingley's family causing more."

"It will not be the Hursts who cause any issues." Jane stopped again, pulling pins out of her mouth. "Rest assured, they have claimed a stance firmly on Mr. Bingley's side in this, and Mr. Darcy's. Mrs. Hurst told me herself, just yesterday, that her husband had given her to understand that she must, if she wishes to maintain a happy household and husband." She popped all the pins but one back between her lips.

"Good." Elizabeth sighed in relief. "I just want to be happy."

"You will be." Jane spoke around the pins again, smiling at her sister for a moment before turning her attention back to Elizabeth's hair. "I daresay there is nothing Miss Bingley can do to turn Mr. Darcy's attention away from you. He is forever staring at you, you know. It is quite amusing sometimes."

Jane winked as she finished pinning the second braid and began to arrange the third.

Elizabeth's eyes looked at the hairpin, but her mind was far away. Her mouth and eyes softened as they remembered Darcy's teasing words and his frequent long stares. She sighed, only coming back to herself when she heard Jane's giggle. She cleared her throat and blushed.

"Were you day-dreaming about Mr. Darcy?" Jane laughed when Elizabeth's blush darkened. "You were!" She stopped what she was doing long enough to wrap an arm around her younger sister's shoulders. She squeezed Elizabeth close and kissed her temple, whispering, "That is so sweet," before letting go. She quickly finished the last braids, allowing the younger girl to get lost again in thoughts of her love.

At long last, Elizabeth and Jane finished their hair and donned their gowns. They scooped up gloves and reticules and pelisses from the end of the bed, slid their feet into their shoes, and headed out the bedchamber door and down the steps. Their father was waiting for them in the entry hall.

"Ah, my early birds are ready to go. The pair of you are always the first to come down." Bennet kissed each daughter on the cheek.

"We are, are we not?" Elizabeth looked at Jane, who gazed back at her with wide eyes. Suddenly, both giggled, covering their mouths with their free hands. A knock on the door startled them.

"That is probably Mr. Darcy and Mr. Bingley. They asked permission to escort you tonight, and I granted it. There will be more room in the carriage for your mother and sisters this way." Bennet turned toward the door, which Mrs. Hill was just opening.

The gentlemen entered the house with a bow for Mr. Bennet and kisses to the hands for Elizabeth and Jane.

"Are you ready to go?" Darcy held his beloved's hand as he asked the question.

"Whenever you are." Elizabeth blushed lightly, knowing she should tug her hand away from Darcy's but not wishing to do so.

"Then, shall we go?" Darcy winked, letting go of Elizabeth's hand and gesturing toward her pelisse. When she handed it to him, he shook it out and held it for her, settling it over her shoulders with a lingering touch. Then, he took her hand again, settling it into the crook of his elbow. He escorted her out the door without checking to see if Bingley and Jane were ready or if Mr. Bennet had any final words for any of them.

Elizabeth laughed. "That was prettily done, Mr. Darcy. You swooped in and carried me off before any of us knew what you were about."

Darcy reddened, but grinned. "You liked that?"

"I think I did." Elizabeth lifted her nose in the air. "I hereby grant you permission to repeat the action at any time in the future."

"Just once?" Darcy laughed at his betrothed's affected air.

"Not just once but any time you wish it." Elizabeth stopped and turned toward Darcy when they reached the carriage. "You are looking forward to this evening."

"Strangely, I am. I do not like being on display, and have little in common with the neighbors here, but I am so very proud to have you on my arm that I find I do not mind being inspected by the four and twenty families in the area." Darcy held his hand out. "My lady?"

With a happy smile, Elizabeth laid her hand in his and allowed him to assist her into the carriage. By this time, Jane and Bingley had arrived; Jane followed her sister into the equipage and sat beside her. Darcy and his friend climbed up in and soon they were off.

The first part of the evening was enjoyable to all, despite Caroline Bingley's clear disdain for the event, its participants, and the reason behind the gathering. There was a brief period of small talk, followed by a meal. Lady Lucas was not as well-versed in social protocol as some hostesses, but she knew Darcy had the highest standing and requested that he and Elizabeth lead the party into the dining room. As guests of honor, he would sit beside his hostess, to her right, and his betrothed would sit beside Sir William, to his right. Darcy, of course, understood protocol and was happy to honor it, but wished with all his heart he could sit beside Elizabeth, as they did at Longbourn. He could see her, as long as no one leaned forward, and that would have to do.

The meal commenced with a soup course. Darcy did his best to take part in the conversation around him. Thankfully, Mr. Bennet was across the table and down one seat, between Jane and Charlotte. He was close enough to direct the conversation away from Lady Lucas' and Mrs. Goulding's preferred topics and toward those Darcy felt adequate to addressing.

The Gouldings' son and heir, Arthur, was on the other side of his mother, also close enough to add to the conversation. Thankfully, he had more sense than his mother.

Darcy looked frequently down the table to stare at Elizabeth. Seated as she was to Sir William's right, she had the elder Mr. Goulding to her right, and Bingley and Mrs. Bennet across from her. She smiled and laughed, and her betrothed soaked it in.

A question from Arthur Goulding brought Darcy's attention back to his end of the table. His reply sparked a debate and he happily defended his position. He had been on the debate team at University. He enjoyed matching wits with others, and Bennet and

Goulding were more than adequate opponents. The ladies, except for Jane, were largely silent. He was a little surprised when one or the other did speak, offering support for one of the gentlemen with a well thought out and concise opinion. *I shall have to amend my opinions of these ladies,* he thought. *Silly they may be, but stupid they are not.*

As the servants exchanged soup bowls for platters of meat, Darcy began to wonder about Caroline. He did not trust her, and though he thought she would probably remain silent in mixed company, it behooved him to be observant and alert as to her whereabouts and actions. Leaning forward and then back, he realized she was on the same side of the table as he was, but nearer to Elizabeth's end. He listened, but was unable to distinguish her voice from any other's. Another long look at his betrothed assured him that Bingley's sister was not causing problems, at least at the moment, so he relaxed and turned his attention again to his tablemates.

Chapter 10

Elizabeth was well aware of Caroline's presence, for she was across the table and two seats down from Mrs. Bennet, between Jerome Tillet and Stephen Lucas. The other woman sent frequent glares down the table, but Elizabeth was not bothered by them. She did notice, however, that partway through the meal, Caroline began to engage Stephen in more conversation than had been her wont previously. Often, she directed his attention toward Elizabeth's section of the table. Looking around, Elizabeth realized that Maria Lucas was on the other side of Mr. Goulding. *Perhaps they are speaking of her,* she thought. *Regardless, I am not going to allow that unhappy woman to ruin my enjoyment of the evening.*

Slowly, the meal rotated through four courses. When the dessert course was finished, Lady Lucas rose, a signal to the other ladies that it was time for them to retire to the drawing room and leave the gentlemen to cigars, port, and male-focused topics of conversation. The ladies all stood and followed their hostess out the door.

In the drawing room, the ladies split up, with Mary sitting down at the pianoforte. The matrons gathered around the fireplace on couches and settees, and the rest sat or stood in groups of two or three.

Elizabeth, having been prevailed upon by her sisters, went to Mary to request she play a specific Christmas carol. With the Yuletide season being so close upon them, Jane, Kitty, and Lydia were certain such a song would be better appreciated than the more somber concerto their middle sister had been practicing for the last few days.

Having completed her mission, Elizabeth was returning to Jane's side when Caroline approached her with a shallow curtsey.

"You have made quite the catch, Miss Eliza, have you not?"

Elizabeth returned Miss Bingley's curtsey with one of her own and smiled. "I am afraid I do not take your meaning."

Caroline's eyes narrowed. "Do not play coy with me. You have somehow snatched up the prize of the century and become engaged to Mr. Darcy. Seriously, though, how long do you think it will last once his relations discover your poor connections and lack of fortune? His uncle is an earl! A divorce would be easy enough for him to manage. He could have anyone, and all he will have to do then is snap his fingers to find a new wife."

One of Elizabeth's brows rose. "And you will be waiting, I assume? To respond to his snapping fingers?" She shook her head. "I think not, Miss Bingley. You do not frighten me. Mr. Darcy and I have already discussed his family and their reactions, and he has assured me of his love and steadfastness. I am not afraid of it suddenly drying up based on circumstances he knew about in advance." She made a move to step past her antagonizer.

Caroline reached out and grabbed Elizabeth's arm. "I do not know how you and your fortune-hunting sister have bewitched both Mr. Darcy and my brother, but I assure you, it will not last. I will see you separated if it is the last thing I do."

Elizabeth shook Caroline's hand off. She stiffened her spine and clenched her teeth, taking a deep breath and letting it out through her nose. "You may feel free to do whatever you think the situation requires, madam, but Mr. Darcy and I will be married in a fortnight. If you wish to be welcomed at Pemberley along with your brothers and sister, you will reconsider your behavior and your words. Good day." Elizabeth stepped around the other woman, marching across the room with her fists clenched at her sides.

Jane had seen her sister's interaction with Caroline, but was too far away to hear anything. When Elizabeth reached her, Jane pulled her close. "Are you well? What did you and Miss Bingley speak about? You seem upset."

Taking another deep, cleansing breath, Elizabeth smoothed her expression and unclenched her jaw. "She tried to threaten me.

She said she would separate me and Mr. Darcy and you and Mr. Bingley."

With wide eyes, Jane looked back at Caroline. "Are you certain that is what she said? Caroline loves her brother; surely she would not wish for his unhappiness."

Elizabeth fought the urge to roll her eyes. "One would think, and yet, those were almost her exact words to me."

"Oh, my." Jane's eyes remained wide. "Perhaps you simply misunderstood her."

Too angry to speak politely, Elizabeth sighed internally and patted her sister's arm. "Perhaps." She turned toward the door as it opened and Sir William strode into the room. "Let us think of more pleasant things for now. I wish to enjoy this evening with my betrothed."

"You are right." Jane's expression brightened when Bingley entered and immediately sought her out. "There are many other things I should like to do."

Elizabeth's eyes glinted with humor to see her sister greet Bingley so warmly. She forced herself to relax as her beloved approached.

"Are you well?" A crease formed between Darcy's brows. "You seem unsettled."

Elizabeth's eye involuntarily strayed to Caroline's location, but she swiftly brought her gaze back to the handsome gentleman standing in front of her. "I am well." She smiled. "Did you enjoy your port?"

Darcy's gaze continued to search Elizabeth's features, the crease between his eyes deepening. "You do not appear well to me. If you are distressed, I should like to know the cause." When her eyes darted to his left again, he followed it, seeing Caroline speaking to Stephen. "Has Miss Bingley said something to you?" His eyes sharpened and caught his betrothed's once more. "You must tell me if she has. Bingley will wish to know."

Elizabeth looked deep into Darcy's eyes, willing him to believe her. "She said nothing important. If I seem distressed, it is only because she was clearly angry. She did not cause a scene; no one else seemed to know we were even speaking together, much less unpleasantly."

"She did say something, though?" When Elizabeth gave him a tired nod, Darcy pressed for more information. "About what?"

"About things you and I have already discussed. I do not wish to speak of it further, if you please." Elizabeth's eyes and jaw tightened, and her lips pinched together.

Darcy paused, examining her closely. "Very well." He reached for her hand and tucked it under his elbow, pressing it tightly to his side. "Come, let us have some tea and find a place to sit down and relax." His lips lifted in a small smile.

Seeing Darcy's attempt to cajole her into a better mood, Elizabeth relented, gracing him with a tiny lift of her lips and allowing him to lead her to the table where a servant was pouring tea, then to a chaise lounge nearby. Settled in with their cups, they began a conversation.

"How did you like your meal?" Elizabeth's eyes glinted.

"I liked it very well. Lady Lucas lays an excellent table." Darcy lifted his tea and took a sip.

"And the conversation? Papa was down at that end, but I could not see who else."

"Your sister, Mrs. Goulding and her son, and Lady Lucas' daughter." Darcy lifted his brows.

"So you were surrounded by a mix of people, some with more sense than others." Elizabeth tilted her head to look at him, then straightened. "You did not answer my query."

"I did enjoy the conversation, as a matter of fact. Some of the ladies might be silly, but they have an underlying intelligence that is not apparent on the surface. We enjoyed a lively debate and they all contributed, including your sister."

Elizabeth's brows shot up. "Jane participated in a debate?"

Darcy nodded, his lips twitching behind his cup. "It was more that she supported her father's position, but yes, she did, as did Lady Lucas and Mrs. Goulding. I daresay it has been a long time since I have had such an enjoyable dinner conversation."

"I am impressed." A pleased smile lit up Elizabeth's countenance. "I am also very happy. It would be a hard thing to love someone who was too arrogant to get along with the people I have known my entire life."

"So all your preconceived notions about me have now been turned on their heads?" Darcy winked when his betrothed laughed. "I caught you out, did I not?"

"You did, you sly thing." Elizabeth's love-filled eyes stared deep into Darcy's. "I do love you, you know."

Darcy swallowed. He glanced around and shifted in his seat, then returned Elizabeth's look. "I love you, as well. I long for us to marry. I do not know how people wait months. The next fortnight could very well be the death of me."

Elizabeth laughed. "Well, we cannot have that."

Just then, Lydia, Kitty, and Maria Lucas loudly prevailed upon Mary for music they could dance to. The Tillet brothers and their cousin had begun moving furniture back.

"It seems we are to have dancing tonight, my love." Darcy set his cup on the table beside the chaise, took Elizabeth's and placed it beside his, then stood. He held out his hand to her. "Shall we join in?"

Elizabeth shook her head but placed her hand in his. "We shall!"

The remainder of the evening was spent dancing with each other and visiting with the other guests. Neither Darcy nor Elizabeth noticed the venomous looks Caroline Bingley frequently threw at them.

~~~***~~~

The next day, Darcy arrived at Longbourn alone. He apologized to Jane on Bingley's behalf.

"He was informed this morning of his sister's words to Elizabeth at last night's dinner. He was too angry to be good company, and he hopes you will forgive him and allow him to visit tomorrow. He plans to invite you all to Netherfield for dinner Tuesday next."

Jane's disappointment in being denied Bingley's company was clear, but as always, her reply was graciousness itself. "You may tell him he is forgiven and that I look forward to seeing him tomorrow."

Darcy took Jane's hand and bowed over it. "On my friend's behalf, I thank you, Miss Bennet. Shall we ask your mother about dinner?" He released her hand, immediately searching for Elizabeth's.

"Shall you ask me what, sir?" Mrs. Bennet's hearing was, at times, selective, but it seemed she was intensely curious as to why
~~~

Bingley had not visited, because she paid close attention to her daughters and Darcy.

"Mr. Bingley is planning a dinner in honor of my engagement to Miss Elizabeth. It is set for Tuesday next and he invites all of you to come. He will be bringing invitations around tomorrow, I believe. His sisters must write them out today."

Mrs. Bennet clapped. "Dinner at Netherfield! Of course, we will come! You may feel free to inform your friend that we look forward to it."

"Excellent." Darcy bowed. "May I be so bold as to request the company of Miss Elizabeth on a walk through the grounds? Perhaps one or two of her sisters would be willing to chaperone?"

"I will go with them." Jane quickly spoke.

"I would rather stay inside today." Kitty covered a cough with her hand. She had not been herself all morning; Jane looked her over carefully, but said nothing.

"I will stay with Kitty." Lydia settled in beside her sister. "Do not worry, Jane, all will be well." She leaned toward the older girl and whispered something to her behind the bonnet she was remaking.

"I will come. I can practice later, and I would like to enjoy the sun while it lasts today." Mary popped up from the table by the window, where she had been writing out extracts.

The party set, the four young people moved into the entry hall, where they retrieved their hats, gloves, and outerwear from the maid. Then, Darcy, with Elizabeth on his arm and Jane and Mary following behind, set out the door.

"Is something wrong with Miss Kitty?"

Elizabeth sighed. "She has a bad cough this morning. It is not unusual for her to be so – at certain times of the year, she coughs and sneezes a great deal – but this time, they seem to be great, deep ones. We are hoping she does not fall seriously ill, as has happened in the past. Jane has set her to drinking tisanes every few hours in the hopes of stopping them before they settle deeper into her and disrupt her breathing."

Darcy's brow creased. "Has that happened often, her breathing being disrupted?"

"It has, unfortunately."

"Would you like me to send for my physician? I would gladly do so. Miss Kitty is soon to be my sister, as well, and I hate to see her fall ill."

Elizabeth squeezed Darcy's arm, gazing up at him adoringly. "Thank you, Mr. Darcy. For now, you do not need to go to such great lengths. Let us see what happens over the next three or four days; if she does not improve, I will let you know and you can send for him."

Chapter 11

By the day of the Bingley dinner, Kitty was perfectly healthy again. Darcy did not need to bring his physician; careful attention from her family and a couple days of rest were all that was needed.

Darcy met Elizabeth at the carriage with an umbrella. The day had turned rainy and cold and he did not wish for her to catch a chill.

"Good evening, my love." Darcy held out his elbow, bracing himself for the spark. Even after touching Elizabeth daily, it still jolted him. It was a sensation he craved.

"Good evening." Elizabeth slid her hand up Darcy's arm, tucking it into the crook of his elbow. With her free hand, she lifted her skirts. "Thank heavens for paved driveways and courtyards. I should hate to have to wade in the mud to go to dinner. The storm came up so quickly this time!"

Darcy lifted his chin. "I promise you, Elizabeth, if the drive was not paved, I would have carried you in." He grinned to hear her laugh.

"Would you, now?" Elizabeth shook her head. They had reached the top of the steps and the covered porch; they paused so Darcy could pass the umbrella to a footman to take down to the other ladies.

"I would. Care for a demonstration?" With a rakish smirk, he bent forward, making Elizabeth squeal and move away.

"Oh, no you do not! You are *not* carrying me." She laughed as Darcy darted toward her.

"Why ever not?" Darcy stretched his arm out.

A throat cleared behind them, startling the couple. "Because you are not yet married." Mr. Bennet gave both of them a stern look.

With deep blushes, Darcy and Elizabeth both murmured apologies. He held his elbow out to her again and when she slid her hand into its place, he led her into the house. He glanced at her as he assisted her out of her pelisse; when she winked, he had all he could do not to laugh out loud. Instead, he limited his comments to a whispered, "Minx!"

Elizabeth and her family were the first of the attendees to arrive. She and Darcy, as well as Bingley, Caroline, and Mr. and Mrs. Bennet would form a receiving line. Since the purpose of the party was to celebrate her and Darcy's engagement, they were expected to greet the rest of the guests in this manner.

Elizabeth was happy to see Charlotte and the rest of the adult members of the Lucas family in attendance. She greeted her oldest friend, as well as Stephen, Maria, and Lady Lucas and Sir William with enthusiasm.

Next to arrive were the Gouldings and Tillets, and they were followed by the Longs. Everyone offered hearty congratulations to Elizabeth and Darcy. By the time the dinner gong had rung, at least one representative from each of the four and twenty families in the area had greeted the couple and wished them well.

The dinner proceeded as all do. Elizabeth thought Caroline was a bit haughty in her behavior toward her guests, but she often was, so Elizabeth shrugged it off. The lady took pains to speak politely to her; it would have to be enough. She and Darcy were separated again, as they had been at Lucas Lodge just a few days before.

Elizabeth looked up and down the long table. Half the guests were seated at this one, with the other half sitting at a second long table behind it. Bingley sat at the end of this table, to her left. Darcy was at the other table, to the right of Caroline. *At least I can see him clearly,* she thought. She noticed Caroline's hand, constantly touching Darcy's arm, and the way he always moved uncomfortably away. *She needs to watch her step. I was serious about her welcome at Pemberley.*

Bingley caught Elizabeth's attention at that moment and for the remainder of the meal, she did her best to focus on her seatmates instead of her hostess.

After eating, the sexes separated as was customary. Elizabeth half expected Caroline to accost her, as she had at Lucas Lodge. Instead, the other woman merely curtseyed shallowly and moved away.

For a full quarter hour, the gentlemen were secluded. Elizabeth circulated amongst the ladies, speaking to everyone and thanking them for celebrating with her. She noticed a servant enter the room and speak to Caroline, and anticipated seeing Darcy.

Elizabeth was surprised a couple minutes later when Caroline approached her. She eyed her hostess warily.

"Good evening, Miss Elizabeth. I hope you are enjoying yourself?" Caroline's voice had a falsely pleasant tone. Her lips barely lifted at the corners.

"I am; thank you." Elizabeth summoned up her most gracious smile.

"I am happy to hear it." Caroline paused as the sound of chairs scraping the floor in the other room filtered through the wall. "The footman informed me that Mr. Darcy asked him to send you a message. He wishes for you to meet him in the garden, near the fountain."

Elizabeth's brows rose. She glanced out at the dark night. The fountain was at the near end of the garden, at the edge of a brick patio. She bit her lip.

"Miss Elizabeth?" Caroline prodded, pulling her guest's attention back to her.

"I apologize. Thank you, Miss Bingley. Did the servant indicate when Mr. Darcy wished to meet me out there?"

"He did not."

Elizabeth thanked her hostess again and walked across the room to the French doors. She opened one and looked out to check the weather. Though chilly, it did not appear to be raining. After another moment of indecision, she stepped out of the house and made her way across the small space to the fountain. "I know he is eager for us to be alone, but this is ridiculous." She lifted her hands to rub her upper arms. Turning, she looked back at the house.

Suddenly, the door opened and a figure stepped through the portal. Elizabeth squinted. It did not appear tall enough to be Darcy. "Who is there?"

"Lizzy? It is Stephen. What are you doing out here?" Sir William's eldest son stopped beside Elizabeth.

"Mr. Darcy sent a message through Miss Bingley to meet him out here. Have you seen him?"

"Did she now? She sent me out here to find you. She said you were distraught." Stephen turned back to look at the house.

"She is up to something, is my guess. We should both go back in." Elizabeth took a step toward the door.

"Yes, I agree." Just as Stephen spoke, the skies opened up with a deluge of rain, instantly soaking both him and Elizabeth. "Now would be a good time."

Elizabeth, with Stephen following, ran to the door and wrenched the handle. It would not turn. "What is this?" She tried again, with no success. She shivered, soaked to the skin by the cold rain.

Stephen put his arm around Elizabeth's shoulder. "Let me try. Come and stand back here." As he reached for the handle, the door flew open and Darcy rushed out.

"Elizabeth?"

"I am here!" Elizabeth ran around Stephen. She stopped short of her betrothed, knowing how the situation probably appeared. "I –"

Darcy did not wait for Elizabeth to explain anything. He immediately pulled her into his embrace. "I did not see you in the drawing room, but I did see Caroline locking this door."

"She told me you asked me to meet you out here." Elizabeth burrowed into Darcy's chest.

"And she asked me to find Lizzy, saying she was distraught and needed a friend." Stephen shook his head. "I should have found you first, but I did not know if you were the reason she was upset. It did not make sense; Lizzy has been angry and sad, but she is never distraught."

"She sent both of you out here, then?" Darcy did not wait for a reply. "She clearly planned something, some sort of compromising circumstance between you, thinking I would abandon Elizabeth." He squeezed his betrothed tighter. "Stupid woman," he muttered. "As if I would ever leave you." He looked down at the shivering lady in his arms. "Come, let us get you inside. I do not want you to catch a cold ten days before our wedding." He turned, leading Elizabeth into the house to the gasps of the other guests.

"Lizzy!" Jane raced to her sister's side. "What happened?" Over her shoulder, she spoke to Bingley, who had followed her. "We need toweling and blankets. Hurry, please."

As Bingley hurried to the nearest servant, Elizabeth was led to a chair positioned in front of the roaring fire with Jane on one side and Darcy on the other. Mrs. Bennet could be heard crying out nearby.

Once Elizabeth was seated and being ministered to by her sister, Darcy straightened, scanning the room. He noticed Caroline using the chaos around her as a cover for an escape and he roared out her name. "Miss Bingley! You will stop now."

Every voice was instantly silenced at the sound of Darcy's.

Bingley was the first to speak. "Caroline? Did you have something to do with this?" He approached his sister, who had frozen in place with every eye upon her.

"She did." Stephen stood from the chair he had been given near Elizabeth's. "She sent Miss Elizabeth outside on a pretext and then sent me out after her, saying Lizzy was upset and in need of a friend."

A gasp rose from the guests. Whispers of "compromise" could be heard.

"Thankfully for us all," Darcy began, "Though I could not find my betrothed, I did see Miss Bingley locking the French doors."

All eyes swung from Darcy back to Caroline.

"I-" Caroline swallowed. She opened her mouth, closed it, and opened it again. When her voice finally worked, it trembled. "I do not know what you are speaking about."

"Caroline ..." Bingley turned red, his fists clenched at his side. A vein began to bulge at his temple.

Louisa suddenly appeared beside her brother. "Perhaps we should deal with this in private."

Gritting his teeth, Bingley nodded.

"You may do as you wish, Bingley, but I intend to make it clear right now that no compromise occurred. Miss Elizabeth is set to marry me in less than a fortnight, and nothing, *nothing* will change that. If I hear one whiff of scandal attached to my betrothed's name, I will know where to look." Darcy stood at his full height, his mien similar to his friend's. "Even if it is not Miss Bingley who ends up being the source, it will have been someone in this room. I will not stop until I have extracted every ounce of recompense from whoever it turns out to be." Darcy stared down every single person in the room who dared meet his eye.

After a long moment of silence in which no one moved, Darcy nodded to Bingley, who began to hustle his sister out of the room while Louisa drew the attention of the rest of the guests to the scheduled entertainment.

Turning back to Elizabeth, Darcy squatted at her side and reached for her hand, which was barely covered by the edge of the blanket. "I am sorry this happened. Promise me you will be well."

Elizabeth shivered but looked him in the eye. "I will be well. I promise."

"Lizzy, we need to get you out of those wet clothes." Jane wrapped a second blanket around her sister.

Darcy stood. "I will ask Mrs. Hurst to make a room available and to provide Elizabeth with a hot bath and a gown."

"Thank you; that will do nicely." Jane smiled at her future brother-in-law, but her eyes were filled with worry.

With a nod, Darcy squeezed Elizabeth's hand once more and then strode across the room. He returned in just a couple minutes. "She has asked the housekeeper to provide whatever Elizabeth needs. By the time we get up the stairs, a room should be ready."

"Good." Jane stood from her position on the floor. "Come, Lizzy. Let us get you up."

Still shivering, Elizabeth stood. The cold wetness combined with the stress of the events that led to her condition and the revelation of Caroline's perfidy, had exhausted her. She swayed.

Darcy had been watching his beloved like a hawk and saw her wobble. Instantly, she was in his arms. Despite her protests, he carried her out of the drawing room and up the stairs, following the flustered Mrs. Nichols into a chamber across the hall from his. He gently placed Elizabeth on the bed, then wiped a strand of wet hair off her cheek and leaned down to kiss her softly. "I will be back to check on you. Your father followed us up. He will want to know what has happened and what will be done about it."

Elizabeth's lips lifted in a wan smile. "I will see you later, then."

With a second, swift kiss, Darcy straightened and went into the hall, pulling the door closed behind him. He spoke briefly to Mr. Bennet, then the two of them descended the stairs to Bingley's study. Darcy knocked on the door, doubting his friend could hear, given the loudness of the argument he was engaged in. With a look at Bennet and a shrug, Darcy opened the door and the two gentlemen slipped in.

Immediately upon seeing his visitors, Bingley stopped speaking. Caroline turned to see what caused her brother to quiet, paling when she saw Darcy's dark visage.

"I apologize, Darcy, on behalf of my whole family. To you, as well, Mr. Bennet." Bingley looked as though he did not know whether to scream or cry.

"None of this was your doing, Bingley." Darcy reassured his friend while glaring at the man's sister. "I am happy that I saw Caroline locking that door and caught on to the scheme so quickly."

"I agree with Mr. Darcy." Bennet strode further into the room, taking up a seat in front of the fire, his scowling eyes never leaving Caroline's face. "I am come to see what punishment you intend to give your sister. Let me warn you, if you do not take care of it, I will. I may not be your family, and I may not have the connections Darcy has, but let me assure you that I *do* have connections to the higher circles."

Chapter 12

The room was silent for a long moment after Bennet made his declaration. The first to speak was Bingley, who cleared his throat and spoke to his sister.

"You see, Caroline? I told you the Bennets were not going to overlook this. You cannot go around arranging the lives of others to suit your tastes. I have already cut off your pin money." Bingley began to pace, running his hands through his hair. "I do not know what else to do to get through that thick brain of yours." He suspended his motion, facing his sister again. "I can tell you that I want you out of Netherfield in the morning. I will speak with Hurst after my guests leave; if he will take you, that would be ideal. If he will not, I will escort you myself." He turned back to Darcy and Bennet. "It should take me no longer than a week to find her a companion and return, if I am still welcome to court Miss Bennet."

Bennet shrugged. "I will leave that to my daughter. I am inclined to grant continued permission as long as you follow through with your sister."

Darcy interrupted. "Georgiana's companion might accommodate you until my wedding. I have already written to my family about bringing my sister here to Netherfield, as we had discussed. I will send a note with you, asking Mrs. Annesley if she will be willing to serve Miss Bingley for a couple weeks. She had hoped to spend the holiday with her daughter in Cheapside."

"Thank you, Darcy." Bingley pressed his palms against his eyes for a moment. "If she will agree to it, I would be appreciative. Perhaps she will know of someone who might serve Caroline permanently?"

Darcy lifted a shoulder. "Perhaps. It will not hurt to ask her. I can inquire of Lady Matlock, as well."

"Thank you; I greatly appreciate that." Bingley turned back to his sister. "Well, there you have it. Your punishment will begin with banishment from my home and this area. Your duty has always been to marry. You will return to town and fulfill that duty. You may remain in the townhouse in London until your marriage, but there will be no shopping, and except for attending soirees where single gentlemen are present and looking for a wife, you will remain at home."

Caroline gasped. "I cannot remain at home and not be out and seen. I will be forgotten by everyone. Invitations will dry up, and I will be left alone."

"Oh, come now, Sister. Louisa will return eventually and she and Hurst may escort you around at that time. When the new season begins and you need a new gown, I will give Hurst the power to approve it."

"*A* new gown?" Caroline's outrage made her flush. "I will need more than one!"

Bingley flicked a finger as though shooing away a gnat. "I do not see why. You have not worn above half what you purchased for this season. You may make one or two over, if you need to." He turned and strode toward the door. "My point, Caroline, is that you must suffer for your actions, and the best way to gain your attention is to take away what you value most. At some point in the future, when I deem you repentant enough, I will revisit this decision." He stepped back to stop in front of his sister. "Trust me when I say, I will need to see evidence of this repentance. If you remain as you are now, defiant and angry, you will never regain your privileges."

Caroline's countenance darkened even more. When she said nothing, her brother spoke again.

"You may begin by apologizing to Darcy and the Bennets. All of them, beginning with Miss Elizabeth and then moving on to Miss Bennet, Mr. Bennet, and Mrs. Bennet, and then the younger girls." Bingley crossed his arms over his chest, his stance wide, and glared at his sister.

Caroline's eyes widened and her jaw dropped as her brother laid out for her his expectations. She began to sputter a reply when a brief knock sounded at the door and the wood panel opened.

Hurst stepped into Bingley's study and took in the expressions of the four occupants. Closing the door behind him, he bowed. "Miss Bennet sent me to inform her father that she wishes to speak to him. Mrs. Bennet has been …" He paused. "Less than helpful, it seems."

Bennet rolled his eyes. "I am sure she has. Thank you, sir. I will attend to her as soon as this current situation is resolved."

Hurst nodded, turning his attention to his brother and sister. "What is our current situation?"

"I am sending Caroline to London. I had hoped to prevail upon you and Louisa to take her, but I can do it myself, if you would rather not. Darcy has offered the services of his sister's companion until we can find one of our own."

Hurst's brows rose. "Giving her her own establishment, are we?"

"Well, she will remain in my townhouse but, yes, for all intents and purposes that is the case. I will remain in charge of her funds, which will be limited. If you agree to take her on, you must approve all purchases for her until I return."

"Hmm; let me discuss it with my wife. I will let you know before we retire."

"Thank you." Bingley returned his attention to Caroline. "I am waiting for the apologies to begin. There is no time like the present, I always say. Best get it done quickly so it is not looming over you."

Caroline gritted her teeth, standing rigidly with her fists clenched at her side. She inhaled through her nose, exhaling noisily. She turned to Darcy. "I apologize."

Darcy blinked. "For what?"

Grinding her teeth harder, Caroline swallowed and then licked her lips. "For trying to destroy your relationship with Miss Elizabeth."

Darcy nodded. "I forgive you. This time. Your welcome at Pemberley will depend upon Elizabeth's desires. Keep that in mind."

Caroline curtseyed to him, then turned to Bennet, mien hard and still flushed. "I apologize for sending your daughter out into the rain and for attempting to compromise her."

Bennet looked Caroline up and down before focusing his gaze on her eyes. After a long moment, and only after she squirmed, he said his piece. "You are forgiven. Your actions are not forgotten, however. Trust, once broken, is difficult to re-establish. In other circumstances, it would not matter, but your brother may one day become my son, which will bring you into my home again. Keep that in mind." He stood from his seat and bowed to the gentlemen. "I will go up now and see what Jane wants." With that, he slipped out the door and up the staircase.

Bingley watched Bennet leave with a thoughtful look. Giving his attention back to

Caroline, he shook his head. "That was a good start, but it was just a start. You owe me and Hurst apologies, and Louisa, as well. If the Bennets are leaving, you may need to write to them. I intend for you to be gone in the morning before they are ready for visitors."

Caroline rolled her eyes and turned away, her hands coming up to rub her arms.

Darcy shook his head at Caroline's actions. "Bingley, you are a good man, and far more patient than I would be." He glanced at Miss Bingley's back once more. "I am going up to see if I can speak to Elizabeth. Let me know what happens after I leave the room. I hope you will return in time to stand up with me at my wedding."

"I would not miss it for the world." Bingley tried to smile, but it was lacking its usual spark. "Thank you for being so forgiving. I know that was difficult."

Darcy looked down. "It is always difficult to forgive someone who hurts the ones I love, but I have to if I wish for my sins to be forgiven me."

"Very true." Bingley murmured the words while giving his sister's back a sad look.

Darcy shook his friend's hand. "I am proud of you. Stay the course, my friend." He bowed to Hurst and to Caroline, who could not see it, then followed Bennet out the door and up the stairs.

When he reached the chamber given to Elizabeth, no one was in the hall outside it, so he knocked.

Jane opened the door. Seeing it was Darcy, she pulled it wider and gestured him in. "Lizzy, Mr. Darcy is here."

Elizabeth sat in front of the fire, her hair in a single long braid over her shoulder, wearing a gown Darcy was sure he had seen on Louisa a few times. He strode to her side, pulling the stool at the vanity over beside the wingback chair his betrothed was in and settling himself on it, flicking his tails back so he did not sit on them. He reached for her hand, holding it between both of his.

"Are you well?"

"I will be." Elizabeth lifted her free hand and ran a finger across his brow. "Do not worry. It was only a chill. I have survived worse."

Darcy used one hand to capture hers as it drifted down his temple. He kissed the fingers, then tucked it back under the blanket that draped her shoulders. "You may have, but never as my betrothed." One side of his lips lifted and fell in a quick smirk. "Worrying about those I love is one of my best-developed skills."

Elizabeth chuckled. "Indeed?" She snuggled her shoulders deeper into the blanket. "I cannot wait to see how this goes." She winked, then grinned when Darcy laughed.

"Minx." He caressed the fingers he held. "Miss Bingley is to apologize to you, to all of you, actually, but it may have to be via letter. Her brother is banishing her from Netherfield. She is to travel back to London in the morning. I am uncertain as of yet who will accompany her; Bingley asked Hurst but might need to take her himself." Darcy glanced up at Jane, who quietly cleaned up the mess they had made. "He has promised to stand up with me, so if he must go, he should only be gone for a week."

"Good; I am glad, for you and for Jane." Elizabeth squeezed Darcy's hand.

Mr. Bennet chose that moment to enter the room. "I have ordered the carriage brought around. Your mother has calmed and will be ready to leave soon." He nodded to Darcy, then looked at his second daughter. "She is well. She has a strong constitution."

Darcy had stood when Elizabeth's father entered the room, but had retained his hold on her hand. "So she tells me." He, along with everyone else, chuckled. "Mrs. Bennet is well?"

With a tired nod, Bennet affirmed it. "Yes. A dose of salts and some individual attention and she is right as rain. You will come to Longbourn and inform me of Miss Bingley's departure?"

"I will. I would imagine we all will feel much better for her leaving. I am sorry her ..." Darcy waved his left hand as though searching for something. "... Fascination with me, or whatever it is, caused Elizabeth grief, and by extension, your entire family."

Bennet shook his head. "It is not your responsibility. I have accepted her apology, weak as it was, but I neither expect nor want one from you. You had no idea what she was up to, and no real harm was done. After the threats you made to the guests tonight, no one around here will dare open their mouths to speculate on the event."

Darcy blushed. "I suppose that was a bit high-handed and arrogant of me. Rather more like my Aunt Catherine or Lord Matlock than I like."

"Be that as it may, I predict it will be highly effective, not to mention the value of the amusement it provided." Bennet chuckled.

"Papa!" Jane and Elizabeth rebuked their father as one. It only served to make him laugh harder.

Elizabeth stood, dropping the blanket to the back of the chair she had been sitting in. "We should go. Mama will be waiting for us." She faced Darcy when he snagged her free hand in his.

"I will escort you to the carriage, and I will visit as soon as I can tomorrow." Darcy lifted one of her hands to his lips, tenderly kissing the back of it. Then, he tucked it under his elbow. "Are you certain you can walk? Shall I carry you?"

"I can walk, thank you." Elizabeth gave him an arch look. "I suspect you would rather carry me, would you not? It gives you an excuse to hold me close."

Darcy sighed. "Yes, and it does." He lifted his chin and sniffed. "However, since I am to be denied that privilege, I must make do with the one I have been granted." He laid his free hand over Elizabeth's fingers where they lay on his arm and caressed them. He led her past her father, who shook with silent laughter, and out the bedroom door.

Chapter 13

The next day, true to his word, Darcy arrived at Longbourn as early as was polite. He entered the drawing room behind Mrs. Hill and waited for the housekeeper to announce him, but his eyes had already sought out Elizabeth. The moment he was free to, he bowed to the Bennet ladies and greeted each of them. Then, he stepped to Elizabeth's side.

"You are well."

Elizabeth laughed. "Is that a question or a command?"

"You look rather more pale than usual." Darcy brow wrinkled as he examined her closely.

Elizabeth sighed. "I confess I do feel rather fatigued. That sometimes makes me appear paler than is my usual wont."

"Sit." Darcy held her hand and eased her down on to the settee. "Have you eaten? Has your sister given you one of her tisanes? Are you warm enough? Perhaps we should sit in front of the fire."

Elizabeth placed her hand on Darcy's arm, urging him to sit beside her. "I have eaten, though it was not much. I have had some herbal tea, yes. Willow bark, I think it was. Nasty stuff, that. I am actually a little chilly, but I can send Mary up to get a shawl and I will be fine."

Darcy stared at her for a long moment, but acquiesced. He arranged himself beside her in such a way that he could see her and his knee touched her thigh. He smiled a little at the blush that reddened her cheek.

"Has Miss Bingley departed?" Elizabeth tilted her head as she looked at him, having sent her sister to fetch her a wrap.

"She did. Just after dawn. Your sister will be relieved to know the Hursts accompanied her." Darcy stood when Bennet entered the room.

"You say Bingley has sent his sister off with the Hursts?" Bennet bowed to his guest before perching himself on a chair.

"I did. He asked me to relay to Miss Bennet that he has business to address today in regards to Miss Bingley – letters that must be written and then sent express – but that he plans to visit on the morrow, if it is acceptable."

Jane let out a breath and clasped her trembling hands in her lap. "You may tell him I look forward to it." She swallowed, then assumed her usual serene expression, though Darcy could see tears gathered in the corners of her eyes.

Elizabeth leaned toward her betrothed. "She was concerned about that. Thank you for easing her mind."

Darcy's brows lifted as he looked at his beloved. "What was she concerned about?"

"She worried that if Mr. Bingley took his sister to London, she would find a way to keep him there. I fear poor Jane's eyes have been opened to Miss Bingley's true nature."

"I am happy to have been of service to her, then." Darcy leaned back. Noting the tea tray being carried into the room by the housekeeper and maid, he spoke to his future father-in-law. "Bingley asked me to apologize to you again on his behalf. He feels terrible that he did not anticipate his sister's actions. I tried to absolve him of the guilt, but ..." Darcy shrugged. "His sense of responsibility is nearly as strong as mine. He would not listen."

"I will write him to stop it." Bennet scooted deeper into his chair, leaning back and twining his fingers together over his midsection. "He must learn to look at these things as momentary diversions designed to amuse him, rather than dire events to be mourned."

Darcy had nothing to reply to that. He was beginning to understand that Elizabeth's father found amusement in everything. It was not something he could understand or participate in.

Soon, the tea had been served and it was time for Darcy to leave. Elizabeth walked him to the door. He would not allow her to escort him all the way to the carriage. "You will stay in where it is dry and warm, and promise you will rest the remainder of the day."

"I promise." Elizabeth wished she could lean against Darcy and enjoy the warmth of his embrace, but it was impossible. "Come back tomorrow and I will be much improved."

Darcy kissed her hand, promised to check in on her the following day, and strode out the door.

~~~***~~~

Two days later, on Friday, an express messenger arrived at Netherfield early in the morning carrying three copies of Elizabeth's settlement. Darcy unfolded them as he broke his fast, silently reading them to assure they said what he wished them to.

Bingley remained quiet, eating his fill while he waited. When Darcy finally murmured to himself and began to fold the pages up again, he spoke. "How do they look?"

Darcy sipped his tea. "Perfect. All that is left is for Mr. Bennet and I to sign them. We will need a witness. I assume you are planning to visit Miss Bennet?"

"I am." Bingley swallowed his bite of food and then picked up his cup. After taking some tea, he finished. "I would be happy to be your witness, as long as Mr. Bennet does not mind."
~~~

"I doubt he cares. Thank you. I will be ready to leave in just a few minutes."

~~~***~~~

An hour later, after a stop at Longbourn's church to purchase a common license, Darcy and Bingley stopped their horses at the bottom of the manor's front steps. A young stable boy ran out to accept the reins, and both gentlemen placed coins in his little palm. They ascended the short staircase and knocked on the door.

"Good afternoon, Mrs. Hill." Darcy tipped his head to her, then removed his hat, gloves, and greatcoat and handed them to her. Bingley followed suit.

"Good afternoon, gentlemen. The ladies are in the drawing room." Mrs. Hill curtseyed.

"How is Miss Elizabeth today?" Darcy knew his betrothed would insist she was well, whether she was or not. The housekeeper was more likely to give him an honest answer.

"Much improved, I would say. She has that sparkle about her again." When Darcy thanked her for the information, Mrs. Hill led the gentlemen to the ladies and announced them.

"Welcome!" Mrs. Bennet was in fine form today, as well, it seemed. "Come, come; do sit down. Mr. Darcy, the wedding plans are coming together quite nicely. The menu has been worked out and," she waved at the tables on
~~~

the side of the room, laden with all manner of ribbons and whatnots, "the decorations are nearly completed. I have set the girls to creating bows for the church pews and centerpieces for the tables, all in blue and white, since it is a winter wedding. I think those colors go perfectly well with the season."

"It all sounds delightful. Thank you for your hard work. You, as well, ladies." Darcy bowed to each of the girls in turn.

Elizabeth grinned to see her betrothed honor her mother and sisters so. She stepped to his side and tugged his arm, leading him away from Mrs. Bennet and to the other side of the room. "That was very well done. More proof that you are not the arrogant fellow everyone thought you to be when you first arrived in Meryton."

Darcy flushed. "Thank you, my love." He helped Elizabeth to sit, then took up a place beside her as close as he dared. "If not for you, I might still seem haughty, you know. You have brought my softer side out."

Elizabeth smiled adoringly at him. "I suspect your true personality would have shown itself one way or another, even had I not come home."

Darcy shrugged. "Perhaps." Not wishing to make the conversation all about him and his flaws, he changed the subject. "My family arrived late last evening. They stayed home at Netherfield this morning to settle in, but they plan to come to Longbourn with me tomorrow, if that is acceptable."

Elizabeth clapped. "Of course, it is! I am eager to meet them, especially your sister."

"She is just as anxious to meet you. I suspect her excitement has kept her from sleeping, and that is why she and our aunt and uncle stayed home today." Darcy chuckled. "I have more good news, if you wish to hear it."

"More?" Elizabeth laughed. "I wish to hear all the good things, so feel free to tell me."

Darcy reached into the pocket of his tailcoat. "Your settlement arrived this morning. I have reviewed it and all looks in order, but I will have your father read it to be certain. I stopped on the way here and purchased the license. Once these papers are signed, all that is left is the wedding next Friday."

"Wonderful! We must take it to Papa, then."

Darcy laughed. "Eager to wed, are you?"

Elizabeth blushed but lifted her chin. "I am. I have no desire to fight off any more ladies and their disappointed hopes."

"I understand. I feel the same. Thankfully, there are no more ladies in Meryton who wish to steal me away, at least none I am aware of." Darcy reached for Elizabeth's hand and squeezed it. "I am just as eager as you, my love." He stood, holding his hand out to her. "Come; let us present this to your father."

Together, the couple presented the documents to Bennet, who, after a quick but thorough perusal, signed all three. Bingley was witness, as promised. Bennet kept one copy, folding it and tucking it into his desk drawer. He handed the other two to Darcy, who tied them up with the ribbon they had come with and slid them back into his pocket.

~~~***~~~

The next day, Darcy brought his family to meet Elizabeth. Though Georgiana was shy, she clearly liked her future sister very much. The younger Bennets overwhelmed her, but she bonded with Mary over the pianoforte.

Mrs. Bennet was far quieter than anyone expected to meet with the earl and countess. She treated them almost reverently, and it fell to Lady Matlock to ease her hostess' nerves.

"You have a fine prospect from the windows in this room. My sister Catherine would say that it is too warm for summer, but the view is worth any amount of heat, in my opinion." The countess smiled warmly at Mrs. Bennet.

"Thank you, my lady. It does get rather warm in here in the hotter months, but we retreat to the back parlor at that time. However, we enjoy this room most of all, and so spend much of our time here."
~~~

"I do not blame you a bit." Lady Matlock looked around. "It is charmingly decorated. Did you do it yourself?"

Mrs. Bennet straightened. "I did, right after I became mistress. It was hard to get Mr. Bennet to agree to it, but he seemed pleased with the changes once they were complete." She looked around. "I would have liked to refresh it before Lizzy married, but Mr. Darcy stressed how important it was to him that you be able to attend his wedding and there simply was not enough time."

Darcy had long before advised his aunt and uncle that he had used their schedules to get the wedding date he wished for, something both had teased him mightily about.

"Sadly, Lord Matlock's position in Parliament limits our flexibility. We are incredibly grateful to you for agreeing to such an early wedding date, and I must compliment you on being able to plan so an important an event so quickly!"

Mrs. Bennet had begun to relax as she spoke to her guest. "Thank you, my lady. It was a challenge, but as Mr. Bennet said, I am talented at pulling soirees together quickly."

"You are! You will have to share with me your secrets."

Later that afternoon, as the Netherfield party returned home, Darcy was happy to hear how much his family enjoyed meeting the Bennets.

"What do you think, Georgiana? Shall you enjoy such a sister?"

Georgiana leaned forward in her seat. "Oh, yes! Miss Elizabeth is everything you said she was. I know she will be so much fun to live with! Miss Mary said she was, and I can see it is true."

Darcy grinned. "Excellent!" He looked at his aunt and uncle. "What did you think?"

"I think Elizabeth is exactly what you need." Lady Matlock's reply was characteristically frank. "She is witty and charming, as well as gracious. She will serve very well as mistress of your homes." She paused. "Mrs. Bennet was not as excitable as you described."

"Elizabeth told me she was awed by your presence. That may change when she sees you again." Darcy shrugged. "I was impressed with her today."

Lord Matlock looked from Darcy to his wife and back. "I enjoyed my time with Mr. Bennet. Very intelligent, that one, though he tends too much toward sarcasm."

Darcy nodded. "That he does. He is rather indolent, as well. I am certain the estate could do better if he were a more involved master."

"It is entailed to the male line, if I remember correctly?" When Darcy confirmed the fact, Lord Matlock continued. "He probably does not see the importance, since his daughters will not inherit. He may have been more involved had there been a son to take over."

"Perhaps. You know who the heir is, do you not?"

The earl shook his head. "No; who is it?"

Darcy smirked, knowing Lord Matlock had visited his sister at Michaelmas. "Lady Catherine's rector."

"That idiot Collins?" The earl snorted. "No wonder Bennet does not care what happens to his estate; with an heir like that, I would let it go, too."

"Henry!" Lady Matlock giggled. "That was rude, but I agree. Mr. Collins was rather singular."

Darcy and the earl laughed heartily at the countess' words, but Georgiana, who had never met Mr. Collins, just looked confused. She shrugged eventually, and looked out the window. The carriage soon pulled to a stop at their destination and she made her way to the music room to practice the song she and Mary planned to play during the wedding breakfast next week.

~~~***~~~

The following days passed quickly. For Elizabeth, there were fittings for her wedding gown, a beautiful, modern design with a very high waist and small sleeves in a pale lilac color. Darcy was kept busy entertaining his
~~~

relatives, including his cousin, Colonel Fitz-william, who had returned to London the day after dropping his parents and ward off at Netherfield and then came back three days before the wedding. The entire party was introduced to the neighborhood, as dinners and balls were held all over the district to celebrate Elizabeth's upcoming marriage.

Finally, the big day arrived. It passed like all weddings do, with vows and prayers spoken, and a sermon preached about marriage and what the new couple could expect. Then, all of Mrs. Bennet's efforts to plan a fantastic wedding breakfast bore fruit. Lady Lucas was suitably jealous, and said so. The guests ate until they could fit no more into their stomachs, and then danced to the music provided by Mary and Georgiana. At the end of the day, Darcy assisted Elizabeth into his traveling coach and off they went for a week in London.

~~~***~~~

On Christmas Eve Day, Darcy and Elizabeth returned to Meryton. Bingley had offered to host them, and they chose to accept. Mrs. Bennet had initially been disappointed, but other events distracted her and all was well.

The newly formed Darcys arrived at Netherfield at noon. Bingley was there to greet them as the coach door opened.
~~~

"Welcome back!" Bingley grinned as he bowed to his friend.

"Thank you." Darcy returned the bow then turned to hand Elizabeth down.

"Ah, Mrs. Darcy, how good it is to see you." Bingley bowed again. "Have you heard from your eldest sister lately?"

Elizabeth curtseyed to Bingley with a laugh. "I have, indeed, my soon-to-be brother. Congratulations."

"Yes, congratulations, Bingley." Darcy shook his host's hand. "Marriage is a wonderful thing. I know you and Miss Bennet will be very happy together."

Bingley grinned, hooking his thumbs in his waistband and rocking back on his heels. "Thank you very much. I know I will be. Jane is an angel; she is everything I ever wanted in a wife." He noticed the footmen walking past with trunks on their shoulders. "Come in, come in. Louisa and Hurst arrived yesterday. She ordered tea the moment we heard your carriage on the drive."

Darcy and Elizabeth looked at each other.

"How is Miss Bingley?" Darcy asked the question, a note of trepidation in his voice.

"In London." Bingley laughed. "Your Mrs. Annesley gave us the name of a lady in straitened circumstances who was looking for a position, I hired her, and Caroline likes her so well that when the lady fell and broke her leg last week, she did not want to leave London without her." He shrugged. "Louisa tells me there is a gentleman who has been calling on her, so that could be part of her reasoning."

Elizabeth's brows rose. "Do tell." She handed her outerwear to Mrs. Nichols, accepting the housekeeper's congratulations with a smile and a few words.

Bingley waited until he had escorted his guests into the drawing room and they had greeted the Hursts before he elaborated.

"His name is Roger Shields. He recently came into his inheritance: an estate in Shropshire worth eight thousand per annum." Bingley perched on the edge of a chair and accepted a cup of tea from his sister. "He is very nearly you, Darcy. Good looking, young, and master of his estate."

"Except he is blonde and short instead of tall and dark." Louisa winked at Elizabeth.

After a bit more time spent catching up, Darcy and his wife retired to the chambers assigned to them to freshen up and rest for a while.

~~~***~~~

That evening, the Netherfield party attended Christmas Eve services with the Bennets. As Elizabeth snuggled as close to Darcy as she could in the cold box, she reflected on the gift she had received – a husband who loved her and who she loved in return. While it
~~~

could not compare to the gift the Christ child made to the world, it was nearly as precious.

Later that night, as she and Darcy cuddled in their bed, she made mention of her feelings. "It is not yet Christmas Day, but this has already been the best holiday season ever. I never would have thought last December that I would be so in love and so very married the next year."

Darcy hugged Elizabeth close, kissing her temple. "I feel the same. It is too late for Jane and Bingley to have a Yuletide wedding as we did, but for the next couple to come along, I highly recommend it."

When Elizabeth giggled, Darcy followed suit. Soon, his kiss silenced her for the night.

Before you go ...

If you enjoyed this book, please consider leaving a review at the store where you purchased it.

Also, consider joining my mailing list by visiting
https://mailchi.mp/ee42ccbc6409/zoeburton
signup

~Zoe

About the Author

Zoe Burton first fell in love with Jane Austen's books in 2010, after seeing the 2005 version of Pride and Prejudice on television. While making her purchases of Miss Austen's novels, she discovered Jane Austen Fan Fiction; soon after that she found websites full of JAFF. Her life has never been the same. She began writing her own stories when she ran out of new ones to read.

Zoe lives in a 100-plus-year-old house in the snow-belt of Ohio with her Boxer, Jasper. She is a former Special Education Teacher, and has a passion for romance in general, Pride and Prejudice in particular, and stock car racing.

Connect with Zoe Burton

Email:
zoe@zoeburton.com

Facebook:
https://www.facebook.com/ZoeBurtonBooks
https://www.facebook.com/groups/BurtonsBabes/

Pinterest:
https://www.pinterest.com/zoeburtonauthor/

Instagram:
https://www.instagram.com/zoeburtonauthor/

Website:
https://zoeburton.com

Join my mailing list:
https://mailchi.mp/ee42ccbc6409/zoeburtonsignup

Support me at Patreon:
https://www.patreon.com/zoeburtonauthor

Me at Austen Authors:
http://austenauthors.net/zoe-burton/

More by Zoe Burton

Regency Single Titles:

I Promise To…

Lilacs & Lavender

Promises Kept

Bits of Ribbon and Lace

Decisions and Consequences

Mr. Darcy's Love

Darcy's Deal

The Essence of Love

Matches Made at Netherfield

Darcy's Perfect Present

Darcy's Surprise Betrothal

To Save Elizabeth

Darcy Overhears

Merry Christmas, Mr. Darcy!

Darcy's Secret Marriage

Darcy's Christmas Compromise

Darcy's Predicament

Darcy's Uneasy Betrothal

Victorian Romance:

A MUCH Later Meeting

WESTERNS:

Darcy's Bodie Mine

Bundles:

Darcy's Adventures

Forced to Wed

Promises

Mr. Darcy Finds Love (available exclusively to newsletter subscribers)

The Darcy Marriage Series Books 1-3

Mr. Darcy, My Hero

Coming Together

Christmas in Meryton

The Darcy Marriage Series:

Darcy's Wife Search

Lady Catherine Impedes

Caroline's Censure

Contemporary Settings:

Darcy's Race to Love

Georgie's Redemption

Darcy's Caution